MacTRUMP

MacTRUMP

*A Shakespearean Tragicomedy
of the Trump Administration, Part I*

BY IAN DOESCHER
AND JACOPO DELLA QUERCIA

Inspired by the work of
WILLIAM SHAKESPEARE

QUIRK BOOKS
PHILADELPHIA

To all the people he afflicted, swindled,
Misrepresented, conned, and tyrannized

Copyright © 2019 by Ian Doescher and Jacopo della Quercia

Library of Congress Cataloging in Publication Number: 2019936672

ISBN: 978-1-68369-160-0

Printed in Canada

Typeset in Sabon
Cover art and interior illustrations by Chloe Cushman
Cover and interior designed by Aurora Parlagreco
Production management by John J. McGurk

Quirk Books
215 Church Street
Philadelphia, PA 19106
quirkbooks.com

10 9 8 7 6 5 4 3 2 1

FOREWORD.

A few words before the show starts: the following is a fictionalized satire of the first two years of the Trump era, which means it's *very* fake. It's not real life, but a deliberate distortion akin to a funhouse mirror, a Snapchat filter, or alternative facts. It takes place in a fictitious world with a wooden core instead of a rocky one. It stars fictional characters—some of them not even human—whose names and personalities we made up as we went along. For example, in our story, Lord MacTrump has two unmarried sons, Donnison and Ericson, who are lovesick dolts *not at all* like their closest approximates. Our characters Prosperosi and Desdivanka enjoy honorific titles for military services never detailed in the play nor analogous to reality. The most advanced technology in our drama is a mirror. The United States does not exist in this play, and never did, but ghosts and monsters do. In short, if any of our characters sound smarter, stupider, similar, or dissimilar to any celebrity or public figure, alive or dead, there's a reason: this book is a parody, and the First Amendment loves protecting parodies that know they belong squarely in the fiction section—which this book surely does.

Some of the events in this drama will be instantly familiar to you. Some might sound real but are taken out of sequence in the context of our deliberately conflated and expanded timeline. Still other moments might make you ask yourself: "Did that really happen?" The answer is probably no, but don't take our word for it. That's what your friends, teachers, libraries, and search engines are for. We wrote this play to provide a glimpse into how a deceased seventeenth-century English playwright might have viewed the world today if forced to live through its present craziness.

As such, please accept this as a work of fiction, a satire, and an homage to the life and writings of William Shakespeare. Enjoy the show!

—THE AUTHORS

DRAMATIS PERSONAE

CHORUS, *across social media*

MacTRUMP, *President of the United Fiefdoms*

LADY MacTRUMP, *his third wife*

DAME DESDIVANKA, *daughter to MacTrump and wife to Lord Kushrew*

DONNISON *and* ERICSON, *sons to MacTrump*

LORD JARED KUSHREW, *husband to Desdivanka*

McTWEET, *a messenger*

STEPHEN BANNOX *and* LADY KELLEYANNE BOLEYN, *advisors*

GARGAMILLER, *a magician*

SEAN SPICERO *and* LADY SARAH PUCKABEE, *heralds*

GRAND DUKE JEFFREY SECESSIONS, *Minister of Justice*

SIR RODNEY ROSENSTERN, *Deputy Minister of Justice*

SIR MICHAEL POMPEII, *Secretary of State*

SIR MICHAEL FLYNNALDO *and* SIR JOHN MacKEELEY, *generals*

PAULUS ROMANAFORT, *a courtier*

MICHAEL LaCÖHEN, *a lawyer*

FOOLIANI, *a fool*

DOCTOR PINO ENOS, *a doctor*

ROGER BLACKSTONE, *a hatchet man*

REINCE PUBIS, *a partisan*

LORD MICHAEL POUND, *Viceroy of the United Fiefdoms*

LADY POUND, *his wife*

SIR ROBERT OF MacMUELLER, *an investigator*

LORD CHIEF JUSTICE JOHN OF ROBERTSON, *Lord President of the High Court*

MITCH MacTUTTLE, GRIMSBY LINDSEYLOCKS, CHARLES
SOOTHER, *and* BERNICARUS, *senators*

LADY NANCY PROSPEROSI, LADY CLEOSANDRIA O'CASSIO,
and SPEAKER PRYAM, *parliamentarians*

BANQUO O'BAMA, GEORGE THE GREATER, BILLIAM O'CLINTON,
GEORGE THE LESSER, RONALD REGAN, RICHARD THE WORST,
DWIGHT D. EISENPOWER, HARRY S. TRUEMAN, FRANKLIN
ROSSEVELT, WILLIAM FALSTAFT, *and* THEODORE ROSSEVELT,
former Presidents of the United Fiefdoms

LORD JOSEPH O'BIDEN, *former Viceroy to O'Bama*

VLAD PUTAIN, *Czar of Prussia*

ROBERT WORMWOOD, *a journalist*

LADY JUSTINE *and* LADY MARIANNE, *progressives and roommates*

JOURNALISTS, SENATORS, PARLIAMENTARIANS, SUPPORTERS,
PROTESTORS, SPECTATORS, GENERALS, ADMIRALS, SOLDIERS,
PILOTS, POLICE, FEDERAL WORKERS, GUARDS, JUDGES,
GHOSTS, TROLLS, BOTS, SNOLLYGOSTERS, GERRYMANDERS,
and OTHER MONSTERS

MacTRUMP

DAME DESDIVANKA

DONNISON & ERICSON

THE GREAT FOOLIANI

McTWEET

Liberty Justice

LADY MARIANNE & LADY JUSTINE

SOOTHER, PROSPEROSI & BERNICARUS

MITCH MacTUTTLE

PROLOGUE.

Washingtown, the United Fiefdoms, in the New World.

Enter CHORUS.

CHORUS   One nation, under God, divides in twain—
Half to the right, their power on the rise,
Half to the left, in fury and disdain—
Two peoples held by aging, fragile ties.
Is this America, which once, so proud,   5
Above the height of lesser nations stood?
How hath there come this overwhelming cloud
To darken freedom's light, so pure and good?
Election, like an axe assaults a stump,
Hath torn the country easily in two.   10
And, from the wreckage, riseth one MacTrump,
Whose government begins with much ado.
If thou hast humor, hear our history,
Which may prove comedy or tragedy.

                                            [Exit.

ACT
I

SCENE 1.

The streets of Washingtown in winter.

Enter McTweet, writing on a scroll
of parchment with a blue quill.

McTWEET   All politics is but a theater,
              And all the politicians merely actors;
              They read their lines and play their fleeting parts
              In pageants we the people judge by vote.
              It hath been dubb'd a great experiment   5
              But is, in truth, a motley entertainment—
              The perfect spectacle in which some knave
              May strut and fret his feathers on the stage
              And single-handedly may steal the show—
              E'en if those hands be orangish and small.   10
                        [McTweet sticks his quill in his cap.
              Such is American democracy,
              The greatest government the world has known.
              At least, 'tis how these actors puff their chests,
              Which I should know, for I am bound to parrot
              Each peep and cheep its rabble tittle-tattles.   15
                        [McTweet reads from several scraps of paper.
              One crow doth cry, "Democracy is humbug,
              A shiny yarn of silken shadow that
              Is puppeteer'd by spiders from dark corners,"
              To which another bustard groans, "The founders
              Were all bad eggs, and their fowl government   20
              As pining, pass'd, and shagg'd as dodos damn'd."

This buzzard pecks at young millennilarks
With sniping hashtags, not with talons sharp.
One night owl older than the dawn of time
Proclaimeth, "Politics is not for chicks,   25
Unless their kind be hooters, tits, or boobies."
Still others—an asylum of cuckoos—
Dumb birdbrains who rely on faux reports,
Whitewash our windows with their fascist facts!
So sings our aviary's jarring choir   30
Of tweeting doves and hawks and eagles bald.
If I thy feathers ruffle, be not peckish—
For I am but a humble messenger,
And 'tis a sin to kill a mockingbird—
Yet such is but a horse of diff'rent feather.   35
My song is ending now, and I must fly—
A new day dawns, the birds again are chirping,
And one enormous cock anon approacheth.

> [*Exit McTweet to rapid drumming.*

Enter SOLDIER. *Drumming continues.*

SOLDIER   Make way for Lord MacTrump!
McTWEET   [*offstage:*]   —MacTrump!
SUPPORTERS   [*offstage:*]   —MacTrump!

Enter more SOLDIERS, *marching with drum and colors.*

SOLDIERS   [*chanting:*] A-thump! A-thump! A-thump, here
                                        comes MacTrump!   40

Enter McTWEET, *also marching.*

ALL   A-thump! A-thump! A-thump, here comes MacTrump!

Enter POLICE, GUARDS, JOURNALISTS, SUPPORTERS,
PROTESTORS, *and* SPECTATORS. *Marching continues.*
MCTWEET *takes and delivers messages throughout the crowd.*

SUPPORTERS   [*singing:*] O beautiful, for spacious skies . . .
PROTESTORS   [*singing:*] We'll not accept his vicious lies!
SPECTATOR 1   I hear his hair was woven out of hay.
McTWEET   Like Doris Johnston and Teresa Nay!   45
SPECTATOR 2   His hands look smaller than an infant boy's.
McTWEET   But not as small as his most fav'rite toys.
PROTESTOR 1   Nay, he was sent here by the devil's grace!
SUPPORTER 1   Thank God for his most upright, Christian base!
JOURNALIST   If any of his speeches have offended—   50
PROTESTOR 2   Go thou to hell, for nothing hath been mended!
ALL   A-thump! A-thump! A-thump, here comes MacTrump!

Enter SENATORS, GENERALS, PARLIAMENTARIANS, *and* MACTRUMP'S
MINISTERS *and* ADVISORS, *including* LADY KELLEYANNE BOLEYN,
who file in and take seats above. Enter LADY JUSTINE, *who
is blind, led by the arm by* LADY MARIANNE. *The two stand
and listen among the* PROTESTORS. *The drumming stops.*

SOLDIER   All hail Lord Michael Pound, who hither comes,
                   Your newfound Viceroy of th'United Fiefdoms!

Enter VICEROY MICHAEL POUND *and* LADY POUND.

SUPPORTERS   Hail! Hail!
PROTESTORS   —Fail!

[Lord Pound and Lady Pound stand and wave.

JUSTINE   —Lesser than MacTrump, yet faker.   55

MARIANNE   One not so sleazy, yet far sketchier.

SOLDIER   All hail to Donnison and Ericson—
Lord men-but-children to our liege MacTrump!

Enter DONNISON *and* ERICSON.

SUPPORTERS   Hail!

PROTESTORS   —Pale!

MARIANNE   —This Ericson looks like a salmon,
A fishy visage with the skin to match.

JUSTINE   Mayhap it is a blessing I am blind.   60

SOLDIER   All hail Lady MacTrump—third wife, first lady!

SUPPORTERS   Hail!

PROTESTORS   —Wail!

McTWEET   *[to Marianne and Justine:]*—Would ye see pictures
of her nude?

MARIANNE   If thou wish'st we shoot not the messenger,
In turn shouldst thou respect her privacy.

JUSTINE   An I could live to see one hundred years,   65
Such nonsense I should never wish to see.

McTWEET   Is that, then, thy reply?

[Marianne takes McTweet's quill
and writes on his parchment.
—"Block'd." Thank you,
ladies!

MARIANNE   Fly hence, thou feather duster. Get thee gone!

[Marianne pokes McTweet with
his quill and he leaves them.

SOLDIER   All hail Dame Desdivanka, daughter to

MacTrump and noble wife unto Lord Kushrew!   70

Enter DAME DESDIVANKA *and* LORD JARED KUSHREW.

SUPPORTERS   Hail!

PROTESTORS   —Jail!

MARIANNE   —What thinkest thou of her, my friend?

JUSTINE   Methinks she is the one we must observe.
Americans, we are a fickle breed—
No other folk more passionately seek
More power, property, and reputation.   75
MacTrump loves her beyond a father's love,
For she is more than daughter: she's his prize.
Her trophy, though, remaineth to be won.

MARIANNE   Then please restrain me from quick judgment, sister.
Without thy wisdom, truly, mine is naught.   80

SOLDIER   All Hail Chief Justice John of Robertson,
Lord President of our esteem'd High Court!

Enter CHIEF JUSTICE JOHN OF ROBERTSON.

PROTESTORS   Fail!

SUPPORTERS   —Double fail!

JUSTINE   —What sentence wouldst thou give
him?

MARIANNE   I have two minds about him, verily,
Yet both are born of woman.

JUSTINE   —Here's a thought: 85
How can we be a land of liberty
If all our laws be slaves to men in robes?

SOLDIER   All rise! [*All stand.*] All hail your sovereign

                                         MacTrump!

                First champion of the Republicons,

                Defeater of the Democrati ranks,   90

                Lord High Commander of the military,

                Defender of the hallow'd Constitution—

McTWEET   [*aside:*] Defender or pretender? Time will tell!

SOLDIER   And president-elect of this, our land,

                Th'United Fiefdoms of America!   95

Enter MacTRUMP.
Both cheers and sobs erupt from the crowd.

SUPPORTERS   Hail!

PROTESTORS   —Heil!

MacTRUMP   —My people, friends and enemies,

                'Tis well that ye have hither come today.

                Forsooth, this is a most tremendous crowd.

                Say Kelleyanne, behold this mighty crowd.

                Was e'er a crowd terrific as this crowd?   100

                It crowds my mind to think upon this crowd.

KELLEYANNE   'Tis passing comprehension, sovereign.

                Thy power is unsinkable—titanic!

MacTRUMP   [*to Kelleyanne:*] Indeed. The biggest crowd there

                                       ever was,

                Which groweth larger ev'ry second, yea?   105

                'Tis unbelievable by ev'ry measure.

                I bid ye, take a picture of the crowd.

                [*To McTweet:*] Take thou a picture.

McTWEET   —Happily, my liege.

[McTweet brings MacTrump a
small painting of the crowd.

MacTRUMP   Take thou a bigger picture, pesky rogue.

[McTweet presents a second, smaller painting.

Whatever. I've no need of such as these.   110

I have my charge as ruler over all—

King of the castle, servant unto none,

Brave keeper of th'United Fiefdoms' might,

Surpassing e'en Hillaria O'Clinton.

The country and its plebians are mine!   115

Bow down before me! I, the great MacTrump!

SUPPORTERS   Hail!

PROTESTORS   —Fail!

ROBERTSON   —Are you prepar'd to take the oath,

The sacred promise of this noble office?

MacTRUMP   More ready am I quickly to get hence—

My stones are freezing. Who hath pick'd this day?   120

Let them be thrown into a dungeon bleak.

ROBERTSON   Good sovereign MacTrump, raise your right hand.

[MacTrump raises his left hand.

Please raise your other hand, my noble liege.

[MacTrump lowers his left hand and raises his
right. Chief Justice Robertson offers him a book.

MacTRUMP   What is this tome thou wavest 'fore my face?

ROBERTSON   A sacred book: the Holy Bible, liege.   125

MacTRUMP   A Bible, eh? Is there no larger book?

ROBERTSON   My lord—

MacTRUMP   —Didst see the one O'Biden had?

'Twas passing yuge. Pray, find me one of those.

ROBERTSON   This Bible once belong'd to Abrahamlet.

MacTRUMP   Then I shall use it, for tradition's sake.   130

	[*aside:*] Though, little good it did for Abrahamlet,
	Who ne'er was president as now I am.
	[*To Robertson:*] Let us commence this pointless rite
	forthwith.
ROBERTSON	Please place your left hand on the Bible, sir.
	[MacTrump takes the Bible with his left
	hand and holds it under his arm.
MacTRUMP	Proceed, proceed! Thou art too slow by half. 135
ROBERTSON	My Lord MacTrump, do you swear solemnly
	And nobly vow to govern all the peoples
	Of each of our United Fiefdoms fifty:
	Of Alabangor, Alaskatchewan—
MacTRUMP	They say that brevity's the soul of wit; 140
	I bid thee be more witty, little John.
ROBERTSON	And all the others fiefdoms, in accord
	With their respective laws and customs?
MacTRUMP	—Sure.
ROBERTSON	Will you preserve, look after, and defend
	The Constitution of th'United Fiefdoms? 145
MacTRUMP	Unto the best of my abilities.
ROBERTSON	So help you God?
MacTRUMP	—So says MacTrump, indeed.
ROBERTSON	Congratulations, Master President.
	[Chief Justice Robertson attempts
	to shake MacTrump's hand.
MacTRUMP	Thy damn hands keep away from royal skin,
	Else thou shalt learn to fear thy president. 150
SOLDIER	All hail MacTrump, thy lord and sovereign,
	And President of these United Fiefdoms!
SUPPORTERS	MacTrump! MacTrump! All hail our liege MacTrump!

[Drums. Ruffles and flourishes. All behind
MacTrump applaud. MacTrump waves at the
supporters and protestors, autographs the Bible,
and throws it at them. It is torn to pieces.

JUSTINE   Hail to your prophet false! Hail to the thief!
MARIANNE   Of doom the harbinger, the evil creep!   155
MacTRUMP   [*aside:*] Now all is mine—the whole world knows
                                                                            MacTrump,
              Which I obtain'd through electoral votes.
              A hostile takeover? Nay, common good.
              When I myself earn'd my first million dollars—
              Sans any aid at all from mine own father,   160
              At least not such as I shall e'er admit—
              I quiver'd at mine own accomplishment.
              When fortune by its zeroes added three,
              And million turn'd to billion, I was proud:
              A self-made man imbu'd with business sense.   165
              Still, something gnaw'd inside me, wanting more.
              I treasure thinking big—I always have.
              To me 'tis very simple: if one shall
              Be thinking anyway, it must be big.
              Most people smaller think, because most people   170
              Are sore afraid to see their own success,
              Afraid of hard decisions, 'fraid of winning—
              Which gives someone like me a great advantage.
              Now I'll go forth among these plebeians
              To speechify as presidents must do   175
              And spout the promises they love to hear:
              [*To all:*] All Washingtown hath flourish'd—but the
                                                                            people
              Did not share in its wealth. The politicians

Have prosper'd—yet jobs fled, whilst fact'ries clos'd.
Th'establishment protected its own self,   180
But not the citizens of our dear country.
[*Aside:*] With platitudes as these their hearts will rise,
They'll shout the name they long for—

SUPPORTERS   —Hail MacTrump!

MACTRUMP   [*aside:*] Yea, now my victory is made complete.
No longer am I merely millionaire,   185
No longer but a meager billionaire,
Now hath MacTrump turn'd president at last.
The flavor of the moment sates my soul.
Alas, though, in a trice the bite turns cold,
Its taste grows bland; I would fain spit it out!   190
What is a president who is elected?
What is an office that may be replac'd?
This is pretense to power, and no more—
I'll not be satisfied until my reign
Endureth past a four- or eight-year span.   195
Putain of Prussia hath the right idea—
Make show of fair elections, with no question
Of competition or the end result.
Or King John Ill, a better model yet—
Whose power pass'd from father unto son,   200
Whose title, supreme leader, speaketh all.
Some flames of envy spark inside my soul—
I'll show that being president is easy,
A task most simple for a man like me.
And then the people—longing to be led   205
By their own noses, e'en as asses are—
Will beg me to remain in power longer,
And hand the reign to others call'd MacTrump.

First, though, unto the speech, and then the ball,
My stomach growls, and I must heed its call.   210
                    [MacTrump exits toward the dais.
                              Exeunt others.

SCENE 2.

The MacTrump inaugural ball.

Enter ROGER BLACKSTONE, LADY KELLEYANNE BOLEYN,
PAULUS ROMANAFORT, *and* SEAN SPICERO, *in evening wear.*
Around them, the banners of the previous president, O'Bama,
are being torn down and paraded. Through the windows
SUPPORTERS *are seen marching with tiki torches.*

ROMANAFORT Huzzah! What an enormous crowd that was!
BLACKSTONE [*smoking a cigar:*] As pump'd and proud as any
                                        morning cock!

SPICERO We could not ask for finer citizens
         As those who fill'd the capital this morning.
         Yea, I saw one supporter in his van,   5
         Festoon'd completely with some tiny portraits
         Of our MacTrump, atop an armor'd tank
         With fireworks and with paper money flank'd.
         Such are the patriots whom we embolden,
         Indeed, the noble spirits we embiggen!   10
KELLEYANNE Ne'er did I doubt attendance on this day
            Would dwarf all others in its size and scope,

                For if election night taught us one thing,
                It's that MacTrump commands a following
                By far more populous than popular.   15

ROMANAFORT   How many of our folk turn'd out today?

KELLEYANNE   As thou well know'st, the numbers do not lie;
                Let us, therefore, engage in doublethink.

SPICERO   'Twas, by my count, twixt one and one million.

KELLEYANNE   We could duckspeak two million at the least,   20
                Or even three, if we were rounding up.

BLACKSTONE   Bah! Sources tell me it was even more—
                Methinks as numerous as five or eight!

ROMANAFORT   Egad! E'en thirteen million persons then?

SPICERO   Such crowd must be unparallel'd! McTweet!   25

         Enter McTWEET *with his pen and parchment.*

                Tell all thy merry magpies that MacTrump
                Hath earn'd a most tremendous victory:
                At least full thirteen million lucky peoples
                Did flock to Washingtown to see his crowning—
                Far more than anyone deem'd possible.   30

McTWEET   [*writing:*] How bullish! Shall I post an image, too?

SPICERO   Nay! Nay to pictures.

ROMANAFORT   —Nyet.

McTWEET   —Are ye so certain?
                A bird's-eye view is being shared e'en now,
                Which makes your mighty host look wafer-thin.
                Especially beside O'Bama's crowd.   35

SPICERO   Thou liest!

BLACKSTONE   —Picture this, deceitful birdie!
         [*Blackstone shows McTweet his rudest finger.*

McTWEET	Pray, wave thy hundred mark not 'fore mine eyes.
KELLEYANNE	To all the naysayers, thou must retweet
	That our unique alternative newfacts
	Are far more factual than actual. 40
McTWEET	[*aside:*] Methinks this will make quite the hashtag.
	#Zounds!
	[*Exit McTweet.*
SPICERO	[*to Kelleyanne:*] I think you think up all the best
	statistics.
KELLEYANNE	I doublethink they be plusgood as well.
ROMANAFORT	Lo! Here comes Bannox and Count Gargamiller!

Enter SIR STEPHEN BANNOX.
Enter GARGAMILLER *from the trapdoor.*

SPICERO	A thousand hails unto the grandest wizards 45
	Who crafted Lord MacTrump's inaugural!
	It was a passing charming incantation.
BANNOX	A thousand Sieg Heils in return. Yet, please,
	Thank me not for the vital words we chose
	To brighten minds before the coming darkness. 50
	Such forces have been decades in the making,
	As well you know, my good Lord Blackstone. Eh?
BLACKSTONE	'Tis true! The harvests we do reap were sown
	In Richard the Worst's southern stratagem.
BANNOX	In sooth, anon we shall embark upon 55
	A trial predetermin'd as the tides
	And as predictable as passing seasons,
	Which bring their summer, autumn, winter, spring.
	Yea, ev'ry nation in this wooden O
	Shares one eight-decades-long experience: 60

A savage growth, a ripe pubescence next,
A retrograde, and then, at last, the fall.
Such was the course of ev'ry empire from
Our nation's founding back to ancient Rome,
And as the fourth great turning fast approacheth 65
So we, too, must embrace the coming darkness
No differently than satanists or Sith.

GARGAMILLER All hail Beèlzebub, the Lord of Flies!
                    [Exit Gargamiller through the trapdoor.

SPICERO Well, then, 'tis well to know you work upon
                    Our noble liege's immigration plan. 70

BANNOX Nay. Gargamiller conjureth that one.

KELLEYANNE E'en Gargamiller?

Enter GARGAMILLER through the trapdoor.

GARGAMILLER   —Speak my name and quake!
                    Our foes, the presses, and the Globe entire
                    Will grow to fear us when that we shall act;
                    Indeed, the powers that MacTrump doth wield 75
                    Are so supreme they may not question'd be!

Enter MACTRUMP, LADY MACTRUMP, VICEROY
MICHAEL POUND, LADY POUND, and GUARDS.

MACTRUMP Who wants to taste O'Bama bubbly?

ALL   —Hail!
                    [MacTrump pops open a Champagne bottle,
                    spraying liquid. Gargamiller hisses and exits
                    through the trapdoor in a puff of smoke.

MACTRUMP I swear, ye'd not believe how many bottles

We have of this fine drink within the White Hold.
'Tis more the pity that the nectar hath 80
Been spent thus far on Democrati losers.
> *[MacTrump drinks from the bottle.*

SPICERO   My liege, methought you shunn'd all alcohol.

MACTRUMP   Newthink again. A thousand quaffs would fail
To sate the thirst that is MacTrump's tonight!

KELLEYANNE   Then to your health, my lord, for as 'tis said, 85
"A drunken lie doth make a sober heart."

BANNOX   Full many blessings on your crown, my lord.
If I may—

BLACKSTONE   [*pointing to the trapdoor:*] —Lord, what was that
demon there?

MACTRUMP   Millerficent?

BANNOX   —Count Gargamiller he.

MACTRUMP   Whatever. Worry not about that man— 90
The guy's most upright and reliable,
He is a mover and a shaker whom
I am most proud to have upon my team.

SPICERO   [*looking up:*] Then wherefore doth he from the
ceiling hang?

MACTRUMP   O, yea? Indeed, he doth from time to time. 95
Methinks it doeth him some good or other.
> *[MacTrump lobs his empty bottle toward the*
> *ceiling. Growls, hisses, and the sound of fabric*
> *tearing can be heard. An O'Bama banner drops*
> *from above. MacTrump hands it to Guard 1.*

MACTRUMP   Throw that atop the bonfires.

GUARD 1   —Yea, my lord.
> *[Exit Guard 1.*

MACTRUMP   Lord Pound, I thank thee for this merriment,

	Thou didst spare no expense for my delight.
POUND	'Tis but frugality, Lord President, 100
	And money well spent on one such as you.
	As once a seer said: take care of the pence,
	And soon the Pounds will take care of themselves.

Enter SOLDIER.

SOLDIER	All hail to General Flynnaldo, who
	Doth lead the loyal forces of MacTrump! 105

Enter GENERAL MICHAEL FLYNNALDO.

ALL	Hail! Hail!
FLYNNALDO	[*kneeling:*]—My liege, I beg your audience.
MacTRUMP	Thou need'st not beg so humbly. Pray, what's up?
FLYNNALDO	[*standing:*] My liege MacTrump, I have a gift for you.
	Behold, your looters found the famous cake
	Serv'd once to Lord O'Bama's smallish crowd 110
	At his far lesser, most pathetic ball.

Enter more GUARDS *carrying a giant cake.*

	There's still is cake aplenty for those here,
	Should you be generous enow to share't.
	Please, take this gift, which is your rightful prize.
MacTRUMP	Well, is this not a sweet surprise? Forsooth! 115
	I thank thee, good Flynnaldo, for thy service.
	As for this trophy, what say you, my public?
	Would ye partake of old O'Bama's cake?
ALL	Yes! Feed us!

MacTRUMP   —What you will. Enjoy your spoils.
                           [A crowd of supporters rushes to the
                                    cake and begins devouring it.

                    Enter GRAND DUKE JEFFREY SECESSIONS,
                    who scurries across the floor, eats several
                           crumbs of cake, and then exits.

ALL   All hail MacTrump!
MacTRUMP   *[to Guard 2:]*   —Take care of this, I pray   120
                    Be sure the plebeians come not too close.
                           [MacTrump shakes hands with supporters
                                    on their way to the giant cake.
                    [To supporters:] Holla. 'Tis well to meet thee. Thou
                                             art welcome.
                    Nay, use no camera. I know. I thank thee.
                    Thank thee for coming to give me thy praise.
                    [To Bannox:] All right, Batshit. What is it that thou
                                             want'st? 125
BANNOX   All thanks, my lord. I hop'd we might discuss
                    Some areas of policy—
MacTRUMP   —O, groan.
                    Pray, step aside, a party is in session;
                    MacTrump shall have his fun ere he doth govern.

               Enter SENATOR GRIMSBY LINDSEYLOCKS, SENATOR
                  MITCH MACTUTTLE, REINCE PUBIS, *and other*
                  REPUBLICON SENATORS *and* PARLIAMENTARIANS.

PUBIS   My lord MacTrump! We were discussing you.   130
MacTRUMP   I'm sure you were, for now I am in charge,

And your charge, ugly suits, is but to work
For me and do my will.
PUBIS   —Yes, well, that is . . .
O! You remember Lord MacTuttle, of
The senatorial Republicons?   135
MacTRUMP   Would that I could forget a face like his.
PUBIS   Of course. Well, he asks—
MacTUTTLE   —Master President,
First and foremost, my full congratulations.
You've done the Party of Republicons
A service grand with your surprise success.   140
MacTRUMP   Tut, tut, vile turtleneck. I did not do
Thou or thy practic'lly embalmèd friends
A favor in November. Nay. I won
Th'election by myself and for myself.
Not one of these, your cronies in the Senate,   145
E'en voted for me, save for good Secessions.

Enter GRAND DUKE JEFFREY SECESSIONS *on his belly.*
He licks MacTrump's shoes and then exits.

MacTUTTLE   Your candor is appreciated, sir,
For in this town it is a quality
That hath grown far too rare. I would not be
Here speaking unto you unless I, too,   150
Believ'd in winning—yea, at any cost.
MacTRUMP   Thou call'st thyself a winner? Art in jest?
Thou traitor who would rob me of election
By stripping Pubis' war chest from my hands!
Thou lookest like the kind of loser who   155
Proceedeth unto church just for the parking.

My pubic hair hath more charisma, wretch!
Thou art a puppet fashion'd from a scrotum.
Is't possible thou call'st thyself a winner?
                    [Exit MacTuttle in dismay. Exeunt
                    Lindseylocks, Pubis, and other Republicon
                    senators and parliamentarians just behind.
Yea, get ye gone, unpleasant huckleberries!   160
Come not to mine inauguration next!

          Enter DAME DESDIVANKA and LORD JARED KUSHREW.

DESDIVANKA   My lord!
MacTRUMP   —Sweet child!
                    [MacTrump pushes Lady MacTrump aside and
                       embraces Desdivanka. They hug and kiss.
MacTRUMP   —How art thou?
DESDIVANKA   —O, my father,
                I saw you speaking with that giant tortoise
                And wanted to approach to give my thanks
                For your decision to divide your prize   165
                With those who would enjoy it more than most,
                And those who do deserve it more than any.
MacTRUMP   O, dulcet daughter, darling, princess fair,
                These fat cats gladly would devour themselves
                Upon that trifle pastry 'til they vomit.   170
                Thou art life's greatest gift, ne'er to be shar'd.
DESDIVANKA   If that be your wish, then, let them eat cake.
MacTRUMP   [to supporters:] You hear that, filthy pigs?
SUPPORTERS   —All hail
                                          MacTrump!
MacTRUMP   What can I do for thee, my dearheart sweet?

DESDIVANKA   My husband and I—

                        [Kushrew waves to MacTrump.

                        —Yea, him over there,   175
            Were talking over all your secretaries,
            And how we thought it would be prudent if—

BANNOX   My lord, as one of those, your secretaries,
            May I suggest you take your daughter's lead,
            Discussing with said secretary—me—   180
            The very subject he deem'd prudent to
            Talk over with you— [*He checks his timepiece.*]

                        —quite some time ago.

MacTRUMP   'Twill not be necessary, Bannerman.
            Thou know'st the whole damn world could turn to
                              dust
            If my belovèd daughter is unhappy.   185
            Tell me, what deem'st thou prudent?

DESDIVANKA   —Father, pray,
            Perforce, it is a topic we may not
            Talk o'er sans some degree of privacy.

MacTRUMP   [*to Bannox:*] Canst make that happen?

                          [Exit Bannox.

            —How is that?

DESDIVANKA   —My thanks.

MacTRUMP   The world entire for thee, my mother's milk.   190
            What is it that thou wishest to discuss?

DESDIVANKA   But this: my brothers and I love you dearly,
            And we believe it would be best if you
            Share freely the suspicions you may have
            Of treachery among your secretaries,   195
            Because you know I never would betray you.
            Instead, I'll proffer you, my lord, my liege,

Whatever help you need, in any way,
To stay above the swamp that doth surround you—
Avoid the slyer demons in our shade.   200

MacTRUMP   I never could doubt thee, my Desdivanka.
Thou art my greatest child, my brightest star,
And I remain in debt to thee—more than
Putain, though I do owe him much as well—
For all the guidance and support thou gav'st   205
Throughout the terrible campaign last year.
Yea, even though I know thou art a friend
Unto the daughter of mine enemy,
Hillaria, the she-beast I did best.

DESDIVANKA   Such friendships are but fleeting, Father dear.   210
You taught me family is more important
Than all the wealth of any bank in Cyprum,
The Payment Islands, Prussia, Switzerloan,
And other undisclos'd offshore locations.

MacTRUMP   You truly have eclips'd me, darling girl.   215
Thou'rt not my equal, nay, thou art my sequel.
And if the gods be good or goddamn'd devils,
I hope to see thee someday take this stage.
                                        [They kiss.

DESDIVANKA   [aside:] Someday. Mayhap on Monday, Tuesday,
                                        Wedn'sday.
Yea, ev'ry dawn and dusk, each day and night   220
Will see the rise of Desdivanka's star.
For, hard as 'twas to win the noble fight
Against Hillaria and her she-troops,
Such was the role the heavens scripted me—
Such was the history I helped abort   225
To see a better woman take her place.

Is it not ev'ry girl or woman's dream
To shatter the glass ceiling, still unbroken?
Have we not all dream'd dreams of being first?
Why should my dream be somehow unbecoming   230
For this, the name the Fates assign'd to me?
Fie! Spit I now on all such petty hatred!
I curse the names and faces of all those
Who scorn my father and my family,
For flaw'd as my impressive house may be,   235
'Tis still my name, my home, my property,
And no one hath the right to take it from me!
This is the lot Lachesis measur'd out
Whilst intertwining me to my poor parents—
As such, the only way I shall achieve   240
My presidential aspirations is
To bind myself unto my father's wheel
And steer his vessel through the coming storm.
He cannot fail. Forsooth, he must not fail.
My future hinges like a door upon   245
His sure success, and if I fail him here,
That door may close fore'er. Such is my mission,
And I shall win the fight, so help me God!
[To MacTrump:] Farewell, kind father. Pray, enjoy
                                        this night,
Which honors thee aright. Lord Kushrew, come!   250
                  [Exeunt Desdivanka and Kushrew.

MacTRUMP   What now? Who comes? A splendid delegation!

              Enter PRUSSIAN DELEGATION.

PRUSSIAN 1   O, President MacTrump, we wish you well.

                    Our greetings are sent from your droog Putain:

                    He doth congratulate you on your win,

                    You and your cheena, e'en Lady MacTrump.   255

MacTRUMP   Pray, tell Putain I shall see him anon,

                    We'll summit as none ever summited.

                    He is a mighty leader, thy Putain—

                    I've never seen the Dems so swiftly muddl'd!

PRUSSIAN 1   He is your servant, waiting on your call.   260

MacTRUMP   [*quietly:*] How go the plans for my new tow'r in

                                           Moskvá?

PRUSSIAN 1   Withdraw from the Assyrian bitva,

                    And then there may occasion be to talk.

MacTRUMP   Then to the Oval Tower we shall flee

                    And there discuss these matters close to me.   265

                    But first, another matter doth arise:

                    I have a bone to pick withal a steak.

                    That, and I straightaway must take a tinkle.

                         [MacTrump hands Lady MacTrump his

                         cake. Exeunt MacTrump in the company of

                         Prussians. Exeunt all but Lady MacTrump.

LADY M.   O, me. The saddest moments are the longest,

                    And this unhappy day stretch'd on for ages.   270

                    Is this to be my newfound normal life?

                    Is't possible this marble city with

                    Its mighty corridors and halls of pow'r

                    Is just another prison, cold as stone?

                           [Lady MacTrump looks down

                                  at her slice of cake.

                    [*To cake:*] Art thou to be mine only company?   275

                    Thou wert here once before, is this not so?

                    Thou wert the cake prepar'd to please the tongue

Of Lord O'Bama! What a charming soul,
A handsome fellow on this dreary day,
A man of inf'nite jest and hopeful outlook,   280
A gentleman crown'd with unequal class,
A sunbeam piercing through the clouds above.
No concept had I of how tall he is
Or how his voice, so deep, would stir my spirit.
E'en thinking on it causeth me to tremble   285
As if mine ev'ry inch were made of glass!
So gentle and so kind was he with me
When we met at the White Hold stairs this morn.
His large, warm hands enfolded my glov'd palm
As if to shield me from the bitter cold.   290
His eyes, so soft and wise, so empathetic,
Seem'd strong enough to gaze upon my soul.
And then, ye gods, there came his tender touch:
Two gentle kisses on cheeks right and left,
Soon follow'd by th'electrifying jolt   295
Loos'd by his strength, enwrapp'd in gentleness,
As he did guide me up the marble steps.
I felt his pull: pure presidential pow'rs!
And when he press'd his hands upon my back,
His fingers twixt the ridges of my spine—   300
God save me, O, I need to sit! [*She sits.*] My
                                          goodness.
So much a man, so much more president.
If but that instant brief could last fore'er,
With he as president, my husband not.
Is that, then, why MacTrump gav'st thou to me?   305
Of course! 'Tis so! He means to tease withal,
For he is envious. I've found him out—

The green-ey'd monster hath infected him!
He's jealous of the bold, superior man
We saw today: that prince, that tall defender,   310
Devoted husband to his only wife.
Sing to me, cake. I pray, enchant me with
The selfsame symphony of sweet sensations
Thou once deliver'dst through his parted lips.
         [Lady MacTrump begins to eat her cake.
Mmm! Yes, pecan! How very tasty—
           [Lady MacTrump accidentally knocks
             the cake off her plate with her fork.
                 —Nay!   315
Do not abscond so soon, my lovely treat!
O, leave me not. Unfold thy memories—
It hath not been five seconds! O, cake, please!
           [Lady MacTrump puts the cake
           back onto the plate, and it falls a
           second time. She exits, sobbing.

SCENE 3.

Outside the MacTrump inaugural ball.

Enter DONNISON *and* ERICSON *severally. Marching is audible
in the distance. Torchlight illuminates the scene.*

DONNISON	What ho, my brother! How is it with thee?
ERICSON	Holla, my eldest sibling, first of friends,

	How can this night be aught but excellent?
DONNISON	The drinks, most plentifully pour'd inside,
	Have stirr'd my blood into a thoughtful flow. 5
	Yea, at the bottom of the flagons deep
	Discover'd I a most reflective mood.
ERICSON	Indeed? What makes thee pensive, brother mine?
DONNISON	Couldst thou have e'er imagin'd what hath pass'd,
	E'er thought our little lives would come to this? 10
	Bethink thee on it, and be thou amaz'd:
	Our father, sovereign o'er all the land,
	And we the rightful princes to his post.
ERICSON	Methinks thou dost not grasp democracy,
	For power doth not travel to the heir, 15
	But rulers fairly are elected. True?
DONNISON	Alack, I am not certain. 'Tis perplexing!
	For George the Elder once hath pass'd his pow'r
	To George the Lesser—when we were young bucks—
	With but a Billiam standing twixt the two. 20
	This Billiam tried to pass his pow'r as well,
	Unto his spouse, Hillaria.
BOTH	—The hag!
ERICSON	Then did our father fittingly prevail,
	And stopp'd those naughty scoundrels in their tracks!
DONNISON	'Tis certain, then, he'll pass the pow'r to us, 25
	For he hath won it honestly and bigly.
ERICSON	A noble, kind, and loving father he.
	Thou, brother, understand'st democracy
	Far better than my younger, simpler self—
	Thou showest all the wisdom of thy years. 30

Enter various SUPPORTERS *carrying tiki torches.*

SUPPORTER 2   The sons of Lord MacTrump! Give them cigars,
And let the smoke ascend to heaven's height,
Wherefrom their mighty father hath descended!

> *[A drumbeat begins. The supporters*
> *break into a tomahawk chop.*

DONNISON   Dear friends, ye are too kind.

ERICSON   —Light up, in joy!

SUPPORTERS   All hail MacTrump!

DONNISON   —MacTrump!

ERICSON   —Hail Chief
MacTrump! 35

> *[Exeunt supporters. Donnison and*
> *Ericson smoke their cigars.*

DONNISON   This life doth suit us well. A worthy game,
Of which we are the rightful champions.

ERICSON   I have not felt this pleasant since the day
When I did slay my first rhinoceros.
How proud I stood beside its ashen frame, 40
Dead from the shots that I adeptly fir'd.

DONNISON   Well I remember! Thou wert so majestic,
Man's triumph over nature on display!
When first I kill'd an elephant, I felt
The selfsame pride thou hadst on that fine day. 45

ERICSON   If thou shalt speak of prides, what of the lions?
Remember when we slew two of a morn?
The strong name of MacTrump was known that day
Across all Africa's savannas.

DONNISON   —Ha!
A mighty vict'ry for two mighty men. 50
I would not have thee think me pompous, brother,
Yet are we two not heroes?

ERICSON   —Yea, and modest—
                  We are the humblest heroes e'er there were.

DONNISON   Our father's vict'ry was more mighty, though:
                  Consider how he hath the foe dispatch'd,   55
                  An 'twere he had her hide within his sights,
                  Crouch'd in the mud and set the perfect trap.

ERICSON   Ne'er was game like Hillaria.

BOTH   —The hag!

                             [They laugh.

DONNISON   Ah, brother, we must share more time together—
                  For after many months apart whilst we   60
                  Did battle in our father's great campaign,
                  This fellowship doth do my spirit good.

ERICSON   Indeed, sweet brother. Perfect men like us—
                  Who are with ev'ry virtue well-endow'd,
                  Which were by our own effort justly earn'd—   65
                  Must stick together in this rough-hewn world.

DONNISON   Thou hast my loyalty unto the end.
                  And yet, there is one thing I feel I lack.

ERICSON   What lack? How can a one as thee know lack?

DONNISON   This is the further cause of my deep thoughts,   70
                  The mood I cannot shake, though all is won.

ERICSON   O, tell me! Bear it not by thine own self!

DONNISON   I almost am afraid to say aloud
                  The matter that doth weigh upon my heart.

ERICSON   My heart is beating through my breastplate! Speak!   75

DONNISON   'Tis love, 'tis love I lack, O Ericson!
                  A woman's love, if I would be exact.

ERICSON   O, Donnison, hath love's cruel fever dreams
                  Bewitch'd you too?

DONNISON   —What spak'st thou, brother mine?

ERICSON   This fortnight past I've lain upon my sheets,   80
                  My lonely heart near howling for a mate.

DONNISON   Thou also, brother? I have shed more tears
                  In these past weeks than in the past nine years,
                  And writ more poetry than I can say
                  Unto celebrity apprentices,   85
                  Emerging but with my love's labor's lost.

ERICSON   Thy verses could not number mine, I'll wager,
                  For I compos'd an epic's worth of lines
                  Unto the ladies pornographical
                  From distant lands I never knew existed.   90
                  O Aphrodite, why won't she love me?
                  I sent her every token that I own'd!

DONNISON   My poems, brother, also speak of her!
                  Thy lady is the object of my verse—
                  The lady who shall love the eldest son!   95

ERICSON   The lady who shall save his younger kin!

DONNISON   The lady who shall tame my fervent heart!

ERICSON   The lady who shall quench my burning flame!

DONNISON   Be joyful, then, for 'tis a sign!

ERICSON   —O . . . brother.
                  Could we two dolts be any more pathetic?   100

DONNISON   Behold the sons of powerful MacTrump—
                  We are but lovesick pups in need of care.

ERICSON   How can it be that neither of us have
                  Found someone who shall love us in return?
                  Yea, love is an elusive woolly mammoth.   105
                  'Mongst ladies I conduct myself correctly;
                  I follow Father's adage: "Grab them by the—"

DONNISON   O, purse thy lips, I too am such a stud!
                  I rival Priapus; yet I've no love.

Belike 'tis politics that ruins ladies,   110
And makes them frigid unto kindly men:
They either speak too much of girly rights,
Or prattle on about inequity.

ERICSON   Or dress in pantsuits built to choke men's loins.

DONNISON   Or some foul combination of those three.   115

ERICSON   Sage words, wise brother, thou hast reason'd well:
Thou couldst a spokesman be for ladyhood,
Since thou dost understand them utterly.

DONNISON   Perchance, young Ericson, this dialogue
We two have shar'd may change our very lives.   120
Both thou and I are sick for love, 'tis so?

ERICSON   Indeed.

DONNISON   —Yet for some cause beyond all sense—
And though we conquer elephants aplenty,
And slay rhinoceroses by the crash,
And overcome e'en lions by our pride,   125
And now our father claims the highest office,
Which shall, in time, be ours by ev'ry right—
We somehow have not captur'd lasses' hearts.

ERICSON   Indeed!

DONNISON   —Then let us, brother, now resolve
To find two ladies we may overcome.   130
We'll undertake our greatest conquest yet!
There's much we two deserve—the world entire—
But loneliness is not our heritage.
If Father can trap not one wife—not two,
But three!—then there are ladies plentiful   135
For Donnison and Ericson to mount
Upon our walls, the trophies of our hunt!

ERICSON   There are, and we shall have them for ourselves.

DONNISON	The hunt begins, and we are ably arm'd!
ERICSON	My thanks, kind brother, for thy rousing words. 140
DONNISON	Come, let us seek some ladies in their herds!

[Exeunt.

SCENE 4.

The Montothello Memorial.

Enter LADY NANCY PROSPEROSI *in a blue
winter cloak, holding her war hammer. Marble columns
surround the temple. At its center, a bronze colossus
stands with its eyes fixed on the White Hold across the
Tidal Pool. The sound of footsteps is heard.*

PROSPEROSI	Who cometh? Whether thou be friend or fiend,
	I bid thee speak thy name and show thy face!

Enter SENATOR CHARLES SOOTHER.

SOOTHER	Bestill your hammer, Lady Prosperosi.
	'Tis but an old and chummy colleague who
	Doth burn with questions and shall warm to
	answers 5
	On this unhappy winter's night.
PROSPEROSI	—My friend,
	I bless thee. Do the other senators
	Know of this midnight conclave that was call'd?

SOOTHER 'Tis just the Democrati tried and true;
The rest are waiting in the wings—they hope 10
And pray MacTuttle somehow grows a soul.

PROSPEROSI My colleagues in the chamber south feel likewise—
They weep for thee and for the future ta'en
When Judge Garlando had his seat denied.
No more with tears; the time for action comes. 15
I trust thy former lord chose these environs?

SOOTHER In faith, Herr Reid did not. Indeed, methought
A secret session had been call'd to order
When I receiv'd the instant message from
A secret sender yet unknown to me. 20

PROSPEROSI As did I, too, but if it was not sent
By neither he nor thou, who is our host?

SOOTHER Aye, there's the rub.

                                     [A clock strikes.

PROSPEROSI   —The time doth turn past midnight.
This day of darkness finisheth at last.

SOOTHER One day down, seventy-three score to go. 25
              [Footsteps are heard from all around.
Dost thou hear that?
              [Prosperosi and Soother take defensive
                     positions at each other's backs.

PROSPEROSI [*to the darkness:*]   —Take heed, approaching villains!
We are the Democrati, who fear naught
But fear itself!

SOOTHER   —Hear, hear! We're not afeard!

The bells go silent. Enter two DEMOCRATI SENATORS.

PROSPEROSI My noble sirs, good even to you.

SENATOR 1	[*bowing:*] —Ma'am.
SOOTHER	Are you alone, or are there others?
SENATOR 2	—Yea—

                                                                                    30

Enter other DEMOCRATI SENATORS.

PROSPEROSI   Say, is this ev'ryone? Have all arriv'd?

Enter SENATOR BERNICARUS.

BERNICARUS   Nay, 'tis not, and I'll tell thee swiftly why:
               This whole clandestine system hath been rigg'd!
               It was design'd by folks like thee to keep   35
               True workhorses like me out of the race!
SOOTHER   My friend, I did invite thee to this conclave.
BERNICARUS   Yet not to lead it! Thou hast come to be
               Too out of touch withal the hoi polloi.
               I give no speeches unto Golden Sacks   40
               Or to—
PROSPEROSI   —Bernicarus! Decorum, please.
BERNICARUS   Who gave thee charge?
SENATOR 3   —Respect our honor'd sister!

The meeting breaks into an argument,
which is interrupted by a whistle. Enter McTWEET *from*
atop the bronze statue, holding a scrap of paper.

McTWEET   [*reading:*] "Birds of a feather should make flock
                                                together."
               That was address'd to all of you, no doubt.
               Good Master Soother, Lady Prosperosi,   45

Ye senators and parliamentarians—
I have a new group message for you all
From he, your former liege, Banquo O'Bama.

SOOTHER   O'Bama plann'd this? Wherefore knew we not?

McTWEET   It was a private group.

PROSPEROSI   —Bird, share his tweet.   50

         [McTweet unrolls a scroll of parchment.

McTWEET   The message reads, "The writing's on the wall."

           [McTweet puts the note away.

PROSPEROSI   And?

McTWEET   —And "The End."

SOOTHER   —Yet is there nothing more?

McTWEET   My use agreement, sir, doth not permit
Me to uncover further information.

           [Exit McTweet.

BERNICARUS   That message was unhelpful in the height!   55
I e'er was disappointed in O'Bama.
He was a bogus Democrato.

SENATOR 3   —Cease!
I understood the meaning of the message,
Which is more literal than metaphor—
We must seek something written on the walls.   60

SENATOR 4   'Tis far too dark.

SENATOR 5   —Hath anyone some flint?

SENATOR 2   I have a stick.

SENATOR 3   —Here's flint.

PROSPEROSI   —Then gather round.

         *[Prosperosi strikes the flint with her
          hammer, creating sparks. The torch
            ignites, illuminating the temple.*

SOOTHER   A sight for sore eyes, by my troth.

SENATOR 3   —Indeed!

BERNICARUS   Behold: the first time in my life I'm speechless.

                     [The Democrati look at the golden lettering
                               covering the walls of the temple.

SENATOR 3   *[reading:]* "We hold these truths to be self-evident   65
                That all men are created equal"—men!—
                "They are endow'd by their Creator with
                Inalienable rights—'mong these are life
                And liberty, pursuit of happiness—
                That to secure these rights have governments   70
                Been instituted in the midst of men . . ."

SENATOR 4   Pray, stop thy reading there. I would not hear
                Of governments rul'd o'er by men right now.

SENATOR 5   Yet 'tis our Declaration!

SOOTHER   —Let it be—
                Thou takest on a losing fight, my friend.   75

BERNICARUS   *[reading:]* "Almighty God created the mind free."
                Yea, free of ruggèd, independent thought,
                If thou ask'st me.

PROSPEROSI   —Nobody asketh thee.

BERNICARUS   And yet 'tis why I spake! For someone must
                Admit that independent thought hath died—   80
                'Tis how MacTrump purloin'd the presidency!

SENATOR 1   'Tis not God's fault thou grow'st more narrow-
                                            minded.

                A noble Democrato would concede
                The race on Super Tuesday, saving face.
                Of course, thou art no Democrato true.   85

BERNICARUS   Forsooth. I'll be goddamn'd before I join
                Thy party!

PROSPEROSI   —Pray, Bernicarus, be silent!

BERNICARUS	'Twas he made mention of the primaries.	
	Shake thou thy silly hammer in his face!	
	I shall have done with this assembly here;	90
	I've neither time nor state of mind. Call me	
	The next time ye elect some crookèd witch.	
PROSPEROSI	Bernicarus, hold thou!	
BERNICARUS	—Nay, I shall fly!	

[Bernicarus stomps away. Soother stops him.

SOOTHER	Pray sir, Bernicarus, a word?	
BERNICARUS	—Not now.	
	My temper doth o'erwhelm my skill with words.	95
SOOTHER	Then listen to me, brother. I pray—nay,	
	I dream—perchance, the day will sometime dawn	
	When bolder Democrati shall elect	
	Another woman as their champion,	
	Or else a man not born of our own race,	100
	Or an adherent to another faith,	
	Or still another choice that is not thee—	
	That thou shalt offer more than muted lips	
	And shirk'd support for weeks and months on end,	
	That thou shalt keep misgivings in thy breast,	105
	And, gracious in defeat, thou'll knowest that	
	To quit the stage with grace and dignity	
	Is, of all things, the utmost difficult.	
BERNICARUS	My friend, an agèd man's a paltry thing,	
	A tattered coat upon a stick, unless	110
	His soul doth clap its hands and sing, and louder	
	For every tatter in its mortal dress.	
	This one I've worn for threescore-fifteen years,	
	Three quarters of a century's expanse.	
	'Tis far too late for me, Bernicarus,	115

To forfeit any shred of soul I have.
A wasted life is not worth living, friend,
A wasted cause not worth defending, either.
So, brother, please, I pray thou wilt permit
Me, at the end, to shuffle off life's stage   120
In th'manner that shall do the greatest good.

          [Exit Bernicarus.

SOOTHER   [*to all:*] Our brother passes, and so doth the hour.
Have we drawn nearer to discovering
The writing that O'Bama referenc'd?

PROSPEROSI   Nay. Naught appeareth to have written been   125
As an addendum.

SOOTHER   —I allot my time
To anyone who wishes to make known
Their honest thoughts of President MacTrump.

SENATOR 1   In that case, I believe he is a bastard
Who driven is by greed and blind with lust.   130

SENATOR 3   I say his lust makes him an easy mark
For enemies abroad who own his all.

SENATOR 4   I fear the safety of th'United Fiefdoms
And for our allies kind, both near and far.

SENATOR 2   Methinks he is our foulest president,   135
As passing racist as his ties are long.

SENATOR 5   He is a symptom of the ills that ail
This nation rather than its leading cause.
MacTuttle rules our chamber cruelly
And any sense of compromise is gone.   140
If government demands two active parties
And only one doth undertake the work,
Then we are like a cart with half a horse.

SENATOR 1   He is the vilest fiend to haunt this land

                 Since pass'd the darkest days of old Jim Crow.   145
The man did slight our former lord O'Bama
With the selfsame perverted energy
As shows a Klansman at a public lynching.
His faith is faker than his golden hair,
And his alliance with the Christian right   150
Doth frighten me e'en as if Lucifer
Climb'd up from hell to conquer heaven with
A wooden ladder form'd of crucifixes.

SENATOR 3   I would hear Prosperosi speak her mind.

SOOTHER   [to Prosperosi:] Bold Madam Speaker?

PROSPEROSI   —Pray, name
                                        me not that. 155
Not yet, at least, until I do deserve't.
We know the oaths that we have taken, friends:
"Support, yea, and defend our Constitution
From enemies both foreign and domestic."
If, then, MacTrump be principal among them,   160
It is our charge to see him punishèd
Unto the fullest measure of the law—
Which meaneth, simply put, by legal means.

SENATOR 2   If thou dost mean impeachment, then thou mayst
Give him thy hammer. Thou didst not impeach   165
When George the Lesser was in office, nay!
So wherefore should we think thou wilt pursue
Such justice in this case?

PROSPEROSI   —Impeachment is
Not in our arsenal, just isn't worth it.
If, soon, Dogcomey and the Deaf Beehive   170
Start buzzing much too closely to MacTrump,
The fool will swat him, which will then unleash

Each faithful agent in the hornet's nest.

SENATOR 2   Canst thou so quickly set aside impeachment,
Which may yet prove our only remedy?   175
And settest thy reliance on Dogcomey,
The mangy dog who doomed Hillaria?
Dogcomey's guilty as Putain the Prussian!

PROSPEROSI   Impeachment for its own sake isn't wise—
It is no remedy, unless removal   180
Doth follow on, which takes the Northern Chamber.
'Til public outcry move th'Republicons,
Impeachment is a sport, and nothing more.
I do not trust Dogcomey any more
Than I may trust MacTrump to rule by law.   185
Yet, still, there is no table big enow
For these two men to share. Pray, mark my words:
Dogcomey or MacTrump cannot both stand—
One domino shall cause the other's fall.

SENATOR 2   That soundeth optimistic to mine ears.   190
The Constitution was not written with
The notion that th'imperfect Deaf Beehive
Would check and balance presidential pow'r.
That charge belongs unto the Parliament,
And it is lost to us. Our allies have   195
Grown fewer and still weaker ev'ry year.
We pride ourselves on our diversity,
Yet our divisions lead to nasty schisms
That the Republicons avoid through faith:
They worship their flaw'd shepherds just as long   200
As they may call themselves part of the flock.
There is no middle ground on such a field.
A certain check against MacTrump requireth

A better, stronger Democrati Party.

SENATOR 5   Hear, hear!

PROSPEROSI   —Indeed, it must be done, for we   205
Are weaker now than e'er. I lov'd O'Bama,
I praise him still. I fought beside him through
Both thick and thin, and brought him victories,
And still I fear that he fell victim to
What Machi'velli warn'd destroyeth those   210
Who hope to rule by dignified example.
It is a wickèd world in which we live—
We're animated by the seven sins
As oceans are, too, by the seven seas.
When he did choose to lead through hope and
                                                virtue 215
Instead of some keen mix of love and fear,
O'Bama set himself up for a fall.
He knew the tools at his disposal, but
He failed to use them due to principles
As paralyzing for a politician   220
As surgeons operating sans a blade.
Th'America o'er which he did preside
Was but a figment of imagination.
In their true form did our United Fiefdoms
Elect MacTrump.

SENATOR 4   —Then, friends, the nation's lost.   225

SOOTHER   Not fully. Like the truths to which we cling,
Our form of government's design'd to bend.
The Constitution doth require ambition
To counteract th'ambition that is flaw'd.
Let's use our flaws much more effectively   230
Than the Republicons.

SENATOR 3	—My friends, behold!
	Methinks I found the message on the wall—
	The one O'Bama hop'd that we would see.
PROSPEROSI	I prithee, sister, raise aloft thy torch.
SENATOR 3	[*reading:*] "I've sworn upon the altar of my God 235
	Eternal enmity against all forms
	Of tyranny over the mind of man."
	So Thomas Jeffersonius did pen
	In 1800, writing to his friend.
SOOTHER	How dost thou know this is th'intended message? 240
SENATOR 3	'Twas th'only one engrav'd upon the wall
	In fewer than one hundred forty char'cters.
SOOTHER	If Jeffersonius and our O'Bama
	Are of the selfsame mind as vile MacTrump,
	Then we must make the people hate him more 245
	Than they hate us.
SENATOR 1	—Speak for thyself, thou imp!
SOOTHER	'Tis true that I am hated, as art thou.
	We could fill up a library of books
	Describing why our party loathes MacTrump.
	Recall, it took a man as ruinous 250
	As George the Lesser for the Democrati
	To galvanize the angry vote that made
	Thee speaker, Lady Prosperosi, yea,
	And let Banquo O'Bama seize the throne.
SENATOR 4	That fiend MacTrump us'd our own plan against
	us! 255
	He made the people hate our rightful lord
	As much as we despisèd George the Lesser.
SOOTHER	Yea. If MacTrump possess'd O'Bama's brain,
	He would have been a formidable foe.

	Yet fortunately, he was born a fool.	260
	We must unite—present a common front—	
	And watch whilst his kakocracy implodes.	
	The Senate for the moment hath been lost,	
	And yet the Southern Chamber is in reach.	
	What thinkest thou, my fearless hammer maiden?	265
PROSPEROSI	The former president—e'en Gerald Fordham—	
	Once said impeachable offenses are	
	Whatever a majority of our	
	Strong Southern Chamber wishes them to be.	
ALL	Hear, hear!	
SOOTHER	—Methinks that solves our mystery.	270
	McTweet!	

Enter McTWEET.

McTWEET	—Yes, sir?	
SOOTHER	—Send thanks to Lord O'Bama.	
McTWEET	It shall be done. Shall I include a picture?	
	[There is scattered nodding among the group.	
	'Tis well! I shall prepare the iObscura.	
	[McTweet runs behind the statue and	
	returns with a large wooden box.	
	Good gentles, be aware: a hashtag call'd	
	The #WomensMarch is trending as we speak.	275
SENATOR 2	Such sounds familiar to mine ears.	
McTWEET	—I'm sure,	
	For sev'ral million women shall attend.	
PROSPEROSI	We must take action in this matter, yea?	
SOOTHER	Hurrah! They'll need a leader! 'Twill be fun.	
	Who'll champion their cause?	

[*All look at one another in silence.*
——Shall anyone?   280
[*Exeunt.*

SCENE 5.

The streets of Washingtown.

Enter WOMEN *marching, shouting, and chanting. Enter* PROTESTORS
wearing pink Phrygian caps. Behind them enter MARIANNE
and JUSTINE *carrying protest signs reading "Liberty" and
"Justice" respectively. Unlike the other women, Marianne wears
a spiked diadem atop her cap and Justine is blindfolded.*

PROTESTORS   [*singing:*] Hark the sound of myriad voices,
                Rising in their might.

ALL   ——In our might!

PROTESTORS   [*singing:*] 'Tis the daughters of the Fiefdoms
                Pleading for the right.

ALL   ——For the right!

PROTESTORS   [*singing:*] Raise the flag and plant the standard,   5
                Wave the signal still.

ALL   ——Wave it still!

PROTESTORS   [*singing:*] Brothers, we must share your freedom,
                Help us, and we will.

ALL   ——And we will!
                [*Marianne and Justine step aside
                to rouse the protestors.*

MARIANNE	[*to protestors:*] Once more unto the streets, women,
	once more!
	Our joy of liberty is half eclips'd! 10
JUSTINE	Be just, and fear not, sisters. Know your rights!
MARIANNE	Make roar, ye lionesses! Show your pride!
	[*All roar.*
MARIANNE	[*to Justine:*] How art thou faring, sister?
JUSTINE	—O, sublime!
	I feel the warmth of souls revitaliz'd
	As if this winter were a summer's day. 15
	A million heartbeats drum against my chest
	Whilst countless footfalls quake my every breath.
	I'm hearing songs of hope instead of rage
	And see how this bold march will trigger change,
	For such a proud display could not have come 20
	Except by justice having been undone.
MARIANNE	Art thou in jest with me, dear sister?
JUSTINE	—Nay!
	My words are true. When justice is besieg'd,
	It rallies noble forces to her aid.
MARIANNE	If only I could see with your mind's eye, 25
	For I perceive a diff'rent, growing threat
	That all our noble systems fail'd to curb
	And all these sister-soldiers could not stop.
	The law is all but toothless in this land
	Against the criminals who break it through 30
	The very means that make it. That is how
	We got MacTrump, and that is why I sense
	Whatever course we take cannot depend
	On systems so corrupted from within.
JUSTINE	But surely thou canst see how dangerous 35

Such sentiments can be. Consider how
MacTrump ascended to his stolen throne—
Without experience in government.
He was a private citizen who spake
Unto a mob who felt as threaten'd by   40
O'Bama as we marchers of MacTrump.
His liberty is full of threats to all,
Be they the government or populace.

MARIANNE   But how can we support a system so
Indebted to injustice since its birth,   45
To slavery and sexism and war?

JUSTINE   Injustice, though within our government,
Is mended by the selfsame engine that
Createth it. If thou wouldst see a foul
Law overturn'd, first see it implemented   50
Unto its full extent. The law shall lose.

MARIANNE   O, fie! I view our laws as spiders' webs:
When any helpless creature stumbles in
They are ensnar'd anon, whilst larger beasts
Break through it and escape without a scratch.   55

JUSTINE   'Tis wherefore spiders make poor senators.

MARIANNE   I say the web was broken from the start;
Our constitution bath'd in vice and greed!

JUSTINE   All forms of justice start from something less,
For justice, sister, is but the composite   60
Of wisdom, fortitude, and temperance
In one harmonious environment.
Their meaner cousin—horrible injustice—
Is born of ignorance, of cowardice
And raw voracity, of unrestrain'd   65
Behavior in the awful forms it takes.

MARIANNE	Yet such behavior makes us human, yea?
JUSTINE	Indeed, which is wherefore I put my faith
	In government oppos'd to none at all.
	What, after all, is government, if not 70
	The greatest self-reflection that we have
	On human nature? If we all were angels,
	No government would necessary be.
	If angels govern'd us, then neither would
	We have a need for government's controls. 75
MARIANNE	Yet what of holy faith, my sister sage?
	Those who'd subvert the public liberty
	Have found essential allies in the clergy.
JUSTINE	A government design'd to safeguard and
	Perpetuate such liberties does not 80
	Demand such mercenaries. If it did,
	Such crutches would become its greatest weakness.
MARIANNE	Methinks that doth explain a lot.
JUSTINE	—It does.
MARIANNE	Ha! O, Justine, if we perchance survive
	This tempest with our liberties intact, 85
	I hope to see thee mistress of its courts.
JUSTINE	And should the scales in that direction tip,
	I hope to ever hold on to thine arm
	As I do now, for thou shalt be my sword.
MARIANNE	And thou my shield. Best friends, forevermore. 90

[They embrace.

Enter McTweet.

McTWEET	[*to all:*] A brief announcement from the president:
	"All peoples of Mohammadian faith

In shathole lands are hereby banned reentry.
Protect the homeland!—hashtag TravelBan."

[All gasp.

PROTESTOR 1   O, shock! Disgraceful!

PROTESTOR 2   —Villainy!

MARIANNE   [to McTweet:]   —What's this?!   95
Doth that include the peoples of Algiers?

[Exit McTweet.

Ah, curses! We should not have blocked him yet.
My parents may affected be by this.
I ne'er may see them! O, what shall I do?

JUSTINE   Be steel, my grand colossus! I'm with thee,   100
And I will help thee fight this harsh injustice.

MARIANNE   Thank you, my sister! I—

[Marianne looks over the outraged crowd.

—I need to speak.

[To protestors:] Is this the legacy we shall pursue,
To lock the doors on those who'd enter in?
Was not our country born of refugees,   105
Of those who immigrated to this land?
Were we not guests once, newly hither come?
Except our native peoples, which of us
Can look back on our ancestors without
Observing immigrants in our proud lines?   110
Some who did choose to see this brave new world,
Some fleeing tyranny in other lands,
Some seiz'd as slaves and forc'd against their will.
MacTrump and his supporters would deny
Our history. They claim to hold aloft   115
The Founding Fathers as their paragons,
Yet gladly twist the meaning of their words.

Religious liberty is promis'd us
Within the Constitution's Bill of Rights,
Not just for Christians white and wealthy, nay—   120
For ev'ryone, regardless of which god
On whom they call, or creed which they believe.
The songs we sing speak to these liberties:
"From ev'ry mountainside, let freedom ring!"
The Statue of our Liberty stands tall   125
To welcome all unto our gracious land.
Remember well the message thereupon,
Proclaiming this: "Give me your tired, your poor,
Your huddled masses yearning to breathe free,
The wretchèd refuse of your teeming shore.   130
Send these, the homeless, tempest-toss'd to me!"
                    [The protestors cheer. Exeunt.

ACT

II

SCENE 1.

Inside the White Hold.

Enter CHORUS.

CHORUS
We the people come out of the cold
As months progress, uncertain and confus'd:
MacTrump doth exercise a stranglehold
On presidential powers, often us'd.
Opponents think, at best, his path's unclear,   5
At worst, that he's a villain spreading woe.
Now Desdivanka plans a move severe—
And sets her sights upon another foe.
Sir James Dogcomey cometh like a pox—
He'd dog MacTrump with harsh investigation.   10
Yet Desdivanka, sly as any fox,
Will ardently protect her father's station.
The plots and schemes most rapidly accrue—
With this, dear friends, beginneth our Act Two.
                              [Exit Chorus.

Enter MacTRUMP.

MacTRUMP
The spring hath sprung, yet I'm stuck in the mud.   15
It's been a disappointment through and through;
E'en daisies are disgusting in my sight.
They spring up for a moment, full of color,
Then die the next day, wither'd by decay.
The floral world is weak and meaningless,   20

And bound on ev'ry side by filthy turds.
Give me, instead, the fields of Mar-Iago:
The luscious turf made for a manly sport,
Where even caddies at their work may dream
Of Cinderella stories on the green,   25
Where ne'er a flower doth disrupt the grounds
Of water features, sand traps, and the rough.
Ah, Mar-Iago—haven to MacTrumps—
How I do miss thy verdant, peaceful leas,
E'en though I travel'd there a fortnight past.   30
Perhaps the springtime still may do me well;
Belike this season's made for my arising,
When I, unlike the daffodil or pansy,
Shall grow into a stronger, manly bud.
Would that I could remove the wretched snakes   35
That slither on my fairway constantly.
The Democrati losers whine and moan,
And little better are Republicons—
Both sides are weak, like flowers to be prun'd,
And I, MacTrump, prepar'd to trim the hedge.   40
I am superior to any bush:
A mighty golfer I, with hardy roots,
Who, with his driver, makes a hole in one,
A firm one-wood beneath my sturdy stump.
Ha, ha! MacTrump the Stump, a virile rhyme.   45
Methinks I am the tee that proudly stood
As frontispiece to Eden's eighteenth hole—
The tee that bore the knowledge of the good
And of the evil, too. Indeed, I know
What good is—I am good at being good—   50
And evil: I'm so good at being evil

That I make evil look like something good.

Enter DAME DESDIVANKA *and* LORD JARED KUSHREW.

	E'en as the words do tumble from my lips,	
	My fav'rite rose in all the world appears:	
	Sweet Desdivank', my blossom and my rosebud.	55
DESDIVANKA	Mine honor'd liege and father most robust,	
	My husband and myself have lately talk'd—	
KUSHREW	The matter, lord, is this—	
DESDIVANKA	—Dear husband, please;	
	The goddess Pallas speaks through silent lips.	
	I hear her singing, "Prithee, hold thy purse,"	60
	For thou hast even failèd to obtain	
	Top-secret clearances to do thy work.	
KUSHREW	Apologies, mine only Desdivanka.	
DESDIVANKA	Forgive th'intrusion of this noisome man—	
	My husband, as you know, he will be talking,	65
	For when the age is in, the wit is out.	
MacTRUMP	Are you not of the same age as he is?	
DESDIVANKA	Nay, Father, he hath full ten months on me.	
MacTRUMP	Ah.	
DESDIVANKA	—Let me start again, third time's the charm:	
	We two were speaking of how we could best	70
	Protect you from your many errant foes.	
	One in particular hath come to mind,	
	Who is, I fear, a taller threat than all.	
MacTRUMP	I would fain know of whom thou speakest, chuck.	
DESDIVANKA	The constable, Sir James Dogcomey he.	75
MacTRUMP	Sir James Dogcomey of the Deaf Beehive,	
	Which doth protect America by stings	

And yet is known worldwide for its discretion?

DESDIVANKA E'en he, the very man. He is a traitor.

MACTRUMP A traitor unto our United Fiefdoms?

DESDIVANKA A traitor unto you, which is the same.
The man doth seek to smear you horridly,
Take your great name and sling his filth upon't,
In hopes that you will fall into disgrace
Withal those whom have long supported you.
He seeks to learn about your Prussian friends—
Those kindly folk who only labor to
Unite the peoples of the world as one—
And how they help'd you unto victory
Against your foe Hillaria.

KUSHREW —Indeed,
'Tis certain that he seeks to do you harm.

DESDIVANKA He'll stop at nothing to besmirch your honor
Unless, brave Father, you do stop him first.

MACTRUMP A snake that hideth in the grass, just so!
Methought I heard a most unpleasant hiss.
More love I cannot shed on thee, my dear,
Yet somehow thou wouldst rise in my esteem
If thou canst tell me how to stop the man.

DESDIVANKA Was the hope drunk wherein you dress'd yourself?
You, sir, are president o'er all the land,
With pow'rs executive that cannot fail.
Employ your fav'rite maxim on the man—

MACTRUMP "I'll have some fries with that"?

DESDIVANKA —Nay, th'other one.

MACTRUMP "You're fir'd."

DESDIVANKA —Forsooth, my father, 'tis the one.
Use that one phrase and let it fall upon

               Dogcomey's head.

MacTRUMP   —If we should fail—

DESDIVANKA   —We won't!

               So screw your courage to the sticking-place,

               For we'll not fail. I trust your fire, bold Father.

               Unleash it on Dogcomey.

MacTRUMP   —So I shall.

               [*Calling out:*] Secessions, Rosenstern, I bid ye

                                            come— 110

               And Bannox, Pubis, ye should hear this, too!

Enter STEPHEN BANNOX, REINCE PUBIS, SIR RODNEY
ROSENSTERN, *and* GRAND DUKE JEFFREY SECESSIONS.

SECESSIONS   What is your bidding, Master?

ROSENSTERN   —Yes, my liege?

MacTRUMP   You two must pen a swift decree for me

               And herald it throughout all Washingtown.

               [*Aside:*] I'll tell McTweet, that he may sing it, too.   115

ROSENSTERN   What shall it say?

MacTRUMP   —Sir James Dogcomey is

               No longer welcome in his current post.

               He must resign, or face his sov'reign's wrath.

                   [*Bannox and Pubis stare at each other.*

ROSENSTERN   My lord, do you believe this plan is wise?

               Dogcomey hath not challeng'd you as yet,   120

               And certainly what he suspecteth of

               Your contacts with the Prussians is untrue.

MacTRUMP   Er, yes. Untrue. And definitely false.

ROSENSTERN   Then wherefore do you need to make this move?

MacTRUMP   O, reason not the need! MacTrump hath spoken,   125

	And thine is not to question why, but do!
	Wouldst thou, mayhap, prefer to share his fate?
ROSENSTERN	Nay, sir, I swear it shall be done.
SECESSIONS	—And swiftly.
	[Exeunt Rosenstern, bowing, and Secessions.
DESDIVANKA	A man, a father, and a president!
	Here, in a trice, you triumph'd at all three.
BANNOX	My lord MacTrump, I'd speak a word with you.
MacTRUMP	What is it, Bantam? 'Tis past time for lunch.
BANNOX	This reckless choice shall wreck you, by my troth.
PUBIS	It is unwise so blatantly to thwart
	Your enemies, e'en if it is your right.
BANNOX	Will this not fuel the fire of foul suspicion?
	Soon all the world will look to Prussia and
	Its interests in you and your young reign.
	Can you not see? Dogcomey is a hydra:
	For each head you remove, two more appear.
DESDIVANKA	Wilt thou, rude man, dispute thy president?
	Do not forget he holds thy strings as well.
MacTRUMP	*[aside:]* She showeth love by her defense of me—
	O Desdivanka, darling of my heart.
BANNOX	My lord, would you vouchsafe me leave to speak
	With your most pleasant daughter privately?
MacTRUMP	She is a grown adult; do as thou wilt.
	In any instance, I must take a leak.
	[Exit MacTrump.
BANNOX	Thou callest me a puppet, little strumpet?
KUSHREW	Forgive me, sir, I shall not stand aside
	Whilst thou insultest—
	[Desdivanka silences Kushrew
	by raising her hand.

Line numbers (right margin): 130, 135, 140, 145, 150

DESDIVANKA   —Do, my faithful husband.
I bid thee sit outside the doorway there,
Whilst I trade words withal this fearsome dragon.

                            [Exit Kushrew.

Thou beggest for this private council, Bannox—
I therefore shall give it to thee in full   155
I understand thine ev'ry motive, toad,
Thou sycophantic flatterer, lickspittle!
Thy mind is mov'd by ancient prejudice
Against myself and my dear husband, Jared.
Forsooth, I spy the way you sneer at him,   160
How thou dost scorn him to the very bone,
How thou wilt never grant him leave to speak
And interrupt his ev'ry thought and word.
At first I thought you envied his good looks
Against that spotted dick thou call'st thy face;   165
Or mayhap thou desir'st his fetching wife,
The blushing damsel standing in thy presence
As ripe for sin as hell is hot with hate.
Indeed, I see through thee like thou art glass,
Because thy rotting skin is paper-thin.   170
Thou hat'st my brilliant husband for the same
Foul reason hat'st thou me: I am a Jew.

BANNOX   Thou silly girl, most overprivileg'd!
Dost thou believe I would—

DESDIVANKA   —I am a Jew!
Dost thou think I shall stand aside, impassive   175
To thy pathetic, paltry prejudice,
Or unaffect'd by thy faux reports?
I am the Jew who did annihilate
The great Fretensis Legion at Masada,

Who once accomplishèd the exile of 180
Nebuchadnezzar unto Babylon,
Who turn'd back Alexander and then Cyrus,
Who flooded seven hills whilst Nero wept!
Thy contribution to this world shall pass
As quickly as a cup of piss doth through 185
The bladder of a man of seventy—

Enter MacTRUMP *and* LORD JARED KUSHREW.

Yet if you e'er insult our faith again,
I swear by ev'ry Jewish bone of mine
I shall unsex thee even where thou standest,
Thou three-inch-member'd, racist, goyish rake! 190
BANNOX   A Jew, you shrew, you lousy screw, 'tis true!
MacTRUMP   What didst thou say, thou horrid bobolyne?
BANNOX   I beg your pardon, lord, for this display,
But these—the members of your family—
Give you advice that should not follow'd be. 195
When you, my lord, remov'd me from the Council
Of National Security, 'twas well—
I ne'er complain'd or aught against you spake.
Yet with this harpy I cannot compete.
Pray, make your choice e'en now: 'tis she or I. 200
MacTRUMP   Bold Bannox, on such footing thou shalt fall.
Ne'er would I choose another o'er my kin,
For she, to me, is like another self,
As if I did upon a mirror gaze
And saw this Desdivanka staring back. 205
She is the strongest, brightest branch upon
The great tree of MacTrump, which standeth proud.

An thou wouldst cut her off so cruelly,
Thou wilt be clipp'd—ne'er was there a decision
As plain as this. Hear, Bannox: thou art fir'd.   210

PUBIS   [*aside*:] O, will it come to this? Imprudent man!
BANNOX   My pride is all I have, which I shall take
                 With me and then depart with utmost haste.
                          [*Exit Bannox, followed by Pubis.*

DESDIVANKA   Twice, Father, you have made me proud today.
MacTRUMP   If I could make a mint by pleasing thee,   215
                 'Twould be the simplest fortune man e'er made.

DESDIVANKA   Forget not, as you go, your maxim, sir.
MacTRUMP   "You're fir'd"? For whom now?
DESDIVANKA   —Nay, the other one.
MacTRUMP   "I'll have some fries with that"?
DESDIVANKA   —You've earn'd them,
                                                      sir—
                 Go to your lunch and fill your belly full.   220
                 Dine happily and dwell upon this thought:
                 You have secur'd your liberty today.
MacTRUMP   I'll have them scallop'd with a cheesy sauce!
                          [*Exit MacTrump.*

KUSHREW   Thou hast done well, my love, and mov'd him to
                 The action thou desir'st: Dogcomey out.   225
DESDIVANKA   Sir James Dogcomey was a canker, which
                 Was necessary to remove at once
                 To help maintain the body politic.
                 Yet his removal was not my main aim,
                 For as a gardener pulls out a weed   230
                 And, in the process, throws away the worm
                 That crawl'd upon the weed, thus wiping out
                 Two pests at once, so both Dogcomey and

The wormlike Bannox promptly are dispos'd.

KUSHREW   Didst thou have Bannox in thine aim as well?   235

DESDIVANKA   Indeed.

KUSHREW   —But wherefore?

DESDIVANKA   —Seest thou not, O imp?

My loving, noble father is a feather

Which may be blown about by any wind.

This Bannox was near bursting with hot air,

Which would have blown my father off his

                                     course— 240

At least, the course on which I'd have him run.

I will not have my schemes undone by him,

Or any other who would cross my path.

'Tis only Desdivanka's squall that shall

Propel MacTrump unto more lofty heights.   245

KUSHREW   Thy craftiness doth move me in my core.

DESDIVANKA   Let's to our chamber, where I'll move thee more.

                                   [Exeunt.

SCENE 2.

Inside the White Hold briefing room
and in the Senate halls.

Enter McTWEET in haste.

McTWEET   Hear ye! Hear ye! Sir James Dogcomey of

The Deaf Beehive is sack'd! The hornet's nest

Is swiftly kick'd, and rumors buzz that all
Of Washingtown has tied themselves in knots
O'er all the threads of tweets at once unfurl'd   5
By a most thunderous MacTrump. They say:
          [McTweet reads from several scraps of paper.
"The Cryin' Senator Chuck Snoozer sobb'd
For he hath lost faith in Dogcomey. Ha!
Then why's he so indignant? #DrainTheSwamp!
The Democrati spake some of the worst   10
Things of Dogcomey, like he should be sack'd,
But now put on an act as players sad!
Dogcomey will soon be replac'd by one
Far better suited for the task to bring
The Deaf Beehive back to its golden self.   15
Dogcomey lost the confidence of all
In Washingtown, both the Republicon
And Democrati fold. When all is calm,
They will be thanking me for what I've done!
One Democrato senator doth speak   20
Of dumb Dogcomey as a jester. Ha!
Methinks the only joker in the deck
Is that defrauding Democrato who . . ."
                    [McTweet turns to another page.
"So falsely sang of how he fought the war
In Vietnuremberg. The ass! He spoke   25
Of bravery and conquests, 'Semper fi!'
To his Connecticutian multitude,
'Til he was caught! The sucker sobbed just like . . ."
                    [McTweet searches for the next page.
[Aside:] We call them tweets, not Twitterstorms,
                                        you know.

[McTweet finds the page and resumes reading.
"A toothless baby, begging for the milk   30
Of human kindness to forgive his fault.
The fraud may think he is my judge and jury,
But he should be the one investigated!
Moreover, those reports on Roger Blackstone
Are C-N-Nothing but pure lies—faux news.   35
I haven't spoken with the goat for days,
And if I did, he never sway'd my hand."
                    [McTweet looks up from the pages.
Was that one hundred forty characters?
Methinks it was a dozen libels more.
                                        [Exit.

Enter SEAN SPICERO *above, on balcony,*
flanked by JOURNALISTS.

SPICERO   Please be ye seated, public enemies.   40
                              [The journalists sit.
First, let me say reports about our border
That tell of children lock'd in unsafe cages
Are wholly false, tell not the tale entire;
For men and women are, too, lock'd therein.
'Tis time for questions, therefore let me ask   45
What can I say that's not already known?
JOURNALIST 1   Perhaps the truth?
SPICERO   —The truth is only this:
The Deputy Attorney General—
Sir Rodney Rosenstern—a man whose record
Is unimpeachable, who has for years   50
Serv'd in the grand department serving justice,

	Who just a fortnight hence hath been confirm'd
	By our United Fiefdoms Senate, yea,
	A vote that was full ninety-four to two:
	This Rosenstern, an honorable man— 55
JOURNALIST 2	Why talk of Rosenstern? Tell of Dogcomey!
SPICERO	This man spake unto his superior,
	Grand Duke Secessions, sharing his opinion
	That this Dogcomey was not fit to serve.
	They shar'd the matter with the president, 60
	Who did, in turn, accept their judgment true.
	Dogcomey was invited to resign.
JOURNALIST 3	Bah! Was not this the bidding of MacTrump?
SPICERO	Nay, never.
JOURNALIST 2	—What of Stephen Bannox, eh?
JOURNALIST 3	Is't true he shall be exiting as well? 65
JOURNALIST 1	Why is th'administration cloak'd in myst'ry?
SPICERO	I bid you, cease. One question at a time.
	[*Aside:*] Alack, I need to find a place to hide!
	Perhaps this stately shrubbery will do.

[Spicero picks up a potted tree
and hides behind it.

JOURNALIST 1	Is that a shrubbery he hides behind? 70
JOURNALIST 2	In faith, it is! And quite a shrubbery.

[Spicero slowly moves away,
hiding behind the plant.

JOURNALIST 1	O, Master Secretary, wherefore do
	You move the trees toward Capitol Hill?
JOURNALIST 2	[*to journalists:*] Come, fellows! We must interview
	that shrub!

[Exit Spicero from balcony,
followed by journalists.

Enter LADY NANCY PROSPEROSI, SENATOR CHARLES
SOOTHER, *and* SENATOR BERNICARUS *below, on stage.*

SOOTHER	Good luck ne'er came with such simplicity! 75
	MacTrump hath sack'd Dogcomey, which shall prove
	His swift undoing in the public eye.
BERNICARUS	If I had been elected, we would not
	Have had to face a farce so ludicrous.
PROSPEROSI	If thou hadst been elected, we would not 80
	Be freezing near this marble colonnade.
BERNICARUS	And if a frog had wings, it would not bump
	Its rear each time it hopp'd along the ground!
	Yet here we are.
SOOTHER	[*to Prosperosi:*] —Canst thou not savor this
	Sweet moment when MacTrump's descent begins? 85
PROSPEROSI	The moment would be easier to cherish
	If we had sturdier assurances.
	The situation, gladly I admit,
	Appears most negative for rank MacTrump—
	Yet he is far more slipp'ry than a snake. 90
SOOTHER	Recall when he said he could stand upon
	The median of Avenue the Fifth,
	And thereupon could shoot somebody down,
	Yet, in the deed, would nary lose a voter?
	Methinks his claim was somewhat justified. 95
BERNICARUS	No thane since Andrew Jacksonstein has said
	Such hateful words more redolent of crime
	And despotism than our nation's ruler.
SOOTHER	[*to Prosperosi:*] Still, thou must feel some measure
	of delight.
PROSPEROSI	A speck, I do confess, of schadenfreude. 100

Enter DEMOCRATO SENATOR I.

SOOTHER	What news?
SENATOR 1	—The rumors we have heard are true—
	Not only hath Dogcomey felt the singe
	Of furious MacTrump's consuming fire,
	But Stephen Bannox, too, doth blaze withal.
PROSPEROSI	E'en Bannox? Is it possible?
SENATOR 1	—Indeed! 105
	Spicero hath admitted to the break,
	And Bannox hath discuss'd the matter freely
	In his appearance on the Pox Network.
PROSPEROSI	The Pox Network! I pray, speak not of it—
	The horrid house of hateful Hannitease. 110
	Enough of poxes. Prithee, dearest Soother,
	Wouldst thou repeat the question thou didst ask
	Of me of late?

          [Soothers pauses, then smiles.

SOOTHER	—If thou shalt savor this
	Sweet moment when MacTrump's descent begins?
PROSPEROSI	Mine answer changeth in a trice: I shall! 115
	The table is arrang'd for perfect service:
	Both Sir Dogcomey and vile Bannox, too!
BERNICARUS	Indeed, it seems our fortunes change forthwith.
SOOTHER	As thou didst forecast, Lady Prosperosi,
	MacTrump hath brought about Dogcomey's fall; 120
	Two men, so proud, could not long coexist.
BERNICARUS	Now Bannox—bankrupt bandleader—is bann'd!
	Did ever news come in such sweet duets?

Enter DEMOCRATO SENATOR 2.

SENATOR 2	Holla, my colleagues—have ye heard the news?
PROSPEROSI	Dogcomey gone?
SOOTHER	—And Bannox out as well? 125
BERNICARUS	Our hopes accomplish'd in a perfect storm?
SENATOR 2	Nay, other news have I: a marshal comes!
PROSPEROSI	Alack, is Prussia pressing their advantage?
BERNICARUS	Shall North Korasia send a missile strike?
SOOTHER	ISISins send guerillas in the midst? 130
SENATOR 2	Nay, nay, ye do misunderstand my news.

                    'Tis not an army come from foreign lands,
                    And neither is it something to be fear'd—
                    At least, not for the Democrati ranks.
                    It is a force not made for battlefields   135
                    But for the battlements of righteousness—
                    A warrior whose steel is but his pen,
                    Whose golden shield is fear'd throughout the land.
                    His armies can win wars without a shot
                    Of firepow'r, save for his indictments apt.   140
                    Sir Rodney Rosenstern hath—in the wake
                    Of innocent Dogcomey's swift dismissal—
                    Us'd his authority to institute . . .

PROSPEROSI	We prithee, speak it out!
SENATOR 2	—An inquisition!

                                          [All gasp.

BERNICARUS	I did not see that coming.
PROSPEROSI	—No one does. 145

        Horns blare. All look to the balcony.
       Enter SIR RODNEY ROSENSTERN *above,*
       on balcony, surrounded by JOURNALISTS.

ROSENSTERN   By virtue of th'authority that hath
              Been vested in mine office, Deputy
              Attorney General, in order to
              Discharge my vast responsibility—
              Providing management and supervision   150
              Of our department serving justice's cause—
              To, thereupon, ensure a full and thorough
              Investigation of the Prussian heads'
              Attempts to interfere in our election,
              I hereby order these three things be done: 155
              Sir Robert of MacMueller is appointed
              As special counsel in the cause of justice,
              The special counsel shall investigate
              The links twixt Prussia and MacTrump's campaign,
              And may, thereafter, prosecute such crimes   160
              Arising from the inquisition's findings.
                        [Horns blare. Exeunt Rosenstern
                                    and journalists.

SOOTHER   Ne'er came an army with a general
              So welcome as this special counsel cometh!
PROSPEROSI   Good news, it seems, is like the trinity,
              Bestowing threefold blessing on us all!   165
SENATOR 1   Methought ye would appreciate this update.
SOOTHER   McTweet, appear!

                      Enter McTweet.

McTWEET   —Thou call'st, and I come flying.
SOOTHER   Canst tell us what the trends are at the moment?
McTWEET   Indeed; if thou say'st, "Squawk," I'll ask, "How
                                              high?"

                          [McTweet checks his parchments.

                      Ah! "'Tis MacMueller time" is on the rise,   170
                      Whilst others call upon "The Lie Detector."
                      Still more revise the MAGA acronym:
                      "MacMueller ainteth going anywhere."

BERNICARUS   Ha! O, you fool, MacTrump. The tweeting birds
                      You gossip with shall hashtag you in jail!   175

PROSPEROSI   With ev'ry piece of news my heart grows fuller.
                      Our liberation comes! Its name: MacMueller.

                                [Exeunt in excitement.

SCENE 3.

Beneath the cherry blossoms at the Tidal Pool.

Enter DONNISON.

DONNISON   The gentlemen whom one first thinks upon
                      When romance is the topic—like, of course,
                      Vindeezel, Schwarzeneggrus, and Stalloni—
                      Were never as turn'd o'er and o'er as my
                      Poor self at even just the thought of love.   5
                      I spend my days in pining for some passion,
                      And nightly weep myself to sleep and hope
                      That I shall dream about a lover's touch.
                      Yet still no ladies break upon my sight
                      Who would approach with amorous intent.   10
                      Would that I might ascend to Mount Olympus,

And thereupon drop in on mighty Zeus—
There was a god who had a way with ladies,
For he did father gods and demigods
In dozens if not hundreds, and each with   15
A diff'rent lady ev'ry single day.
Once I had talk'd with Zeus and learn'd his ways,
Then I would go to visit Cupid next—
The man-boy thing who hath the flappy wings—
And tell him to release an arrow—nay,   20
A quiver's worth of arrows, by my troth!—
Upon my lonely body presently:
Romantic acupuncture, verily,
Which would ensure I'd get a lady soon.
This loneliness hath lasted far too long,   25
Its pain too deep, its harshness too severe,
For Donnison to carry on much more.
Soon, I must either meet my future bride
Or wither like potatoes on the vine.
Behold this landscape, made for love to bloom—   30
The cherry trees that blossom pink and white
And drop their gentle leaves upon the ground,
Creating an exquisite promenade.
Ne'er was a heart so fill'd with love as mine,
Awaiting a receptacle most fair   35
In which my dripping love may gently flow.
                              [*He begins to weep.*

        Enter DAME DESDIVANKA, *unnoticed.*

DESDIVANKA   What's this? My elder brother in a grove
              And blubbing with unmanly sniffles? Bah!

I would be worried if methought he wept
For reasons consequential to myself.   40
And yet, mine instincts give me cause to wonder:
What could disrupt my simple sib so much
That he should shed the robes of dignity
By weeping nakedly upon the earth?
The wolves of Washingtown have many eyes,   45
Which e'er are fix'd upon my softer brothers,
Awaiting any opportunity
To slander the MacTrumps with false reports.
I will not let such shameful spectacles
Embarrass Father and disrupt my plots.   50
I, therefore, shall observe my brother here
To guarantee the dolt betrays me not.
                    [*She hides behind a monument.*

DONNISON   O, is this not a pitiable sight?
To all the world, it seems I've ev'rything—
My father president, and I his courtier.   55
Yet still the tears fall, springing from mine eyes,
An 'twere a waterfall cascading grief.
But soft, I spy my brother drawing near—
I'll hide myself 'til I no longer weep.
                    [*He hides behind a tree.*

                    Enter ERICSON.

ERICSON   [*singing:*] If she be single, I shall woo,   60
If she be pretty, bring her, too,
If she be smart, she'll have to do,
                    Sing nonny for the ladies.
If she be farmer, I shall moo,

If she be Kanga, I'm her Roo,   65
If she be married, I am blue,
   Sing nonny for the ladies.

DONNISON   [*aside:*] At least in heartsickness I have a peer.

                                                [*Donnison emerges.*

Good day, young Ericson.

ERICSON   —O! Donnison,
Didst thou behold me as I hither stroll'd?   70
Methinks, perhaps, I should be most embarrass'd—

DONNISON   Nay, do not fret. I heard thy ballad, yea,
Yet would not mock thee for the world entire—
Indeed, it mov'd my soul to hear thee sing,
For I, of late, have wistfully been walking   75
And dreaming of an unknown paramour.

DESDIVANKA   [*aside, hidden:*] A pair of milksops—both do bring
                                  me shame!

ERICSON   We are two fools.

DONNISON   —Two fools beset by love
And its o'erwhelming power o'er our lives.

ERICSON   What shall we do?

Enter LADY JUSTINE *and* LADY MARIANNE
walking, not seeing the boys.

MARIANNE   [*to Justine:*]   —The cherry blossoms bloom.   80

JUSTINE   Mine eyes have not the strength to view the sight,
But pause—the fragrances are beauteous.

DONNISON   [*aside to Ericson:*] O brother, see the maidens sweet
                                and gentle—
An instant answer to our fervent pray'rs!

ERICSON   [*aside to Donnison:*] Like angels come from heaven,
                                 by my troth!   85

MARIANNE   [*to Justine:*] Didst hear the news about MacMueller's
                                 probe?

JUSTINE   I did! And if MacTrump hath aught to hide,
It won't elude a bloodhound like MacMueller.
The scales of justice tilt in our direction!

MARIANNE   Then shall the people have their liberty   90
From all the villain's foul maneuverings!

DESDIVANKA   [*aside, hidden:*] See how my brothers' mouths do
                               fall and gape
As they behold the simple women here.
These harlots revel in my father's fall!
Should either of my brothers try to lure   95
These wenches with a boast, I fear the wreck
Their siren song could bring if they do learn
The secrets known within the House MacTrump.
                [*Exeunt Justine and Marianne.*

DONNISON   [*to Ericson:*] Hurrah! Our perseverance is rewarded!
So long we've waited for love to appear—   100

ERICSON   And suddenly it comes in double form.
One each for both of us! Which one lik'st thou?

DONNISON   What is the difference? For they are ladies!
We shall divide the spoils once they are ours.
How shall we win them?

ERICSON   —Let's devise a plan.   105
                [*Donnison and Ericson step
                   aside and talk privately.*

DESDIVANKA   [*aside, hidden:*] I cannot watch these lummoxes for
                                 long.
I shall distract them with a cunning ruse—

Yet not alone. McTweet!

Enter McTweet, *unseen by the boys.*

McTWEET   —My maiden fair,
I hear thine orisons! How may I serve?

DESDIVANKA   Two new accounts I would create posthaste   110
The first call'd "Mistress Quickly's Girls" and th'other
"Besotted Betty."

McTWEET   —Sorry, that one's taken.

DESDIVANKA   Then "Debbie Doth DC."

McTWEET   —A frightful play,
Not one of Marlowe's best, an thou ask'st me.

DESDIVANKA   I shall use both accounts for messages.   115
Anon, my brothers shall be sending missives
Unto the monikers. Canst thou do this?

McTWEET   Yea, false accounts, ma'am, are my specialty.

DESDIVANKA   Once they reply, I bid thee forward on
Their messages to one another. See?   120
One shall respond, yet it shall seem as though
The message cometh from the other woman.
Then, not a single errant word they share
Will make its way into mischievous hands!
Dost understand?

McTWEET   —Their thoughts pass'd on by bots, 125
I comprehend and shall fulfill my task.

DESDIVANKA   Then to thy work, good bird, and I to mine.
        [*Desdivanka pulls the quill from McTweet's cap
        and pens a message. She hands it to McTweet.
        Donnison and Ericson's conversation is
        interrupted when McTweet whistles.*

DONNISON   What's this? A message cometh suddenly.

                       [McTweet hands the message to Donnison.

ERICSON   Aught with our father? Are we needed back?

DONNISON   Nay, nay, 'tis from one "Mistress Quickly's Girls."   130

ERICSON   Confounding, verily. What doth it say?

DONNISON   [*reading:*] "My friend and I just pass'd thee and thy
                                         brother,
               Whilst we did walk among the cherry trees.
               I recognize thee from the Pox Network.
               I hope it is not far too forward, sir,   135
               But I would meet with thee. Alone. At night."

ERICSON   Is't possible?

DONNISON   —This, brother, must be fate!

               [Desdivanka motions to McTweet. He whistles
                    again and when the boys are distracted,
                       McTweet snatches the message from
                       Donnison's hand and gives it to Ericson.

ERICSON   A message comes for me as well—ha, ha!
               From "Debbie Doth DC"—a classy name.

DONNISON   She soundeth friendly. Pray, what doth it say?   140

ERICSON   [*reading:*] "My friend and I just pass'd thee and thy
                                           brother,
               Whilst we did walk among the cherry trees.
               I recognize thee from the Pox Network.
               I hope it is not far too forward, sir,
               But I would meet with thee. Alone. At night."   145

DESDIVANKA   [*aside, hidden:*] Two shrewder men than these two
                               pigeon eggs
               Would realize that the words are all the same.
               Yet these buffoons are so adrift in lust
               That copy/paste should suit their simple minds.

ERICSON   Our plan to woo the ladies is not needed—   150
                 Behold, they circle round like moths to light!
DONNISON   The gods above have listen'd to our pleas
                 And, in a trice, have done their very best.
ERICSON   Let's step aside and answer.
DONNISON   —Yea, at once!
                 We shall not keep love waiting at the door.   155
                        [Donnison and Ericson step away
                        from each other to respond privately.
                        McTweet pulls out two quills from his
                        satchel and hands one to each boy.

                 Enter SIR ROBERT OF MACMUELLER, aside,
                 flanked by DEAF BEEKEEPERS in black robes.
                 They are hidden and watching the brothers,
                 swinging thuribles that emit smoke.

MacMUELLER   [to beekeepers:] What's this? Some secret messages
                                                     are sent?
BEEKEEPER 1   [pointing off:] There may be more where that came
                                                from, my master.
MacMUELLER   I see. Let us, then, spy on what's abuzz.
ERICSON   [writing:] Belovèd creature, I would meet thee soon.
                        [He hands the message to McTweet, who
                        pretends to pocket it, but carries it to
                        Donnison and delivers it to him. Donnison
                        reads it, delighted, and writes back.
DONNISON   [writing:] Thou art more beautiful than all the world. 160
                        [Donnison hands this message to McTweet,
                        who takes it to Ericson. The scene continues

                 in such manner, McTweet passing between the
                 two boys quickly while they are unaware.

ERICSON   [*writing:*] Nay, thou art even more so, I declare.

DONNISON   [*writing:*] Where shall we meet?

ERICSON   [*writing:*]   —Belike the Tow'r
                                        MacTrump?

DONNISON   [*writing:*] A worthy place for romance, by my troth.

ERICSON   [*writing:*] Methinks it is the perfect place to meet
                 When one would be discreet and secretive.   165

DONNISON   [*writing:*] I cannot wait to be discreet with thee.

ERICSON   [*writing:*] I will take off thy clothes with utmost speed.

DONNISON   [*writing:*] O darling, I do burn with primal lust.

ERICSON   [*writing:*] Shall I send thee a picture, which shall whet
                 Thy hearty appetite for carnal pleasures?   170

DONNISON   [*writing:*] Most gladly would I view it, by my troth,
                 Yet, sadly, should not through this messenger,
                 For, I admit, my father frequents him.

ERICSON   [*writing:*] O, 'tis no cause for shame, my life, my
                                          love—
                 My father also hath me on his plan.   175

DONNISON   [*writing:*] This day shall live forever in my heart—
                 The day thou didst slide into my DMs.

ERICSON   [*writing:*] Let us meet soon. Tonight. At eight o'clock?

DONNISON   [*writing:*] The Tow'r MacTrump! I'll thither fly on
                                          wings.

ERICSON   [*writing:*] Farewell for now, my lovely, wondrous
                                          one! 180

McTWEET   [*aside, panting:*] Exhausting work, to catch two birds
                                          at once!
                     [Exit McTweet. Donnison and
                           Ericson reconvene.

DONNISON	How goes it?
ERICSON	—Better than I could expect!
DONNISON	For me as well.
ERICSON	—Indeed?
DONNISON	—We meet tonight!
ERICSON	Huzzah! So shall I with my lady, too!
DONNISON	We are the most deserving men I know. 185
ERICSON	This could not happen to two better men.
DONNISON	Let's go have lunch to celebrate this day.
	Love makes me hungry for some mead.
ERICSON	—Lead on!

[Exeunt Donnison and Ericson.
Desdivanka steps out of hiding.

DESDIVANKA	Ha! This was better than I could imagine!
	Were ever there such fools as my two brothers? 190
	Though I have plots and intrigues far more vital,
	I'm certain I've nipp'd this one in the bud.
	I shall make way to Tow'r MacTrump tonight
	To see these lovesick blockheads hang their heads
	When they see neither woman doth appear. 195
	Not since the Prussians met us secretly
	To talk about Hillaria have I
	Been so excited for a meeting there!

[Exit Desdivanka. MacMueller
steps out of hiding.

MacMUELLER	From wicked ways a secret doth arise—
	From humor shall be born humility. 200
	A secret meeting with the Prussians, eh?
	For some discussion of Hillaria?
	These matters I shall swiftly follow up.
	It is my priv'lege to investigate,

To strive for justice and protect our nation.   205
Our doctrine I pursue most heartily:
Fidelity, brav'ry, integrity.
      [Exeunt MacMueller and beekeepers.

ACT
III

SCENE 1.

In the Oval Tower.

Enter CHORUS.

CHORUS Time trips along as though the state were drunk
And fumbling home along a darken'd road.
MacMueller, like a solitary monk,
Works quietly beneath a mounting load.
Our play's too short to hold the vast expanse   5
And share the many tales that would enthrall—
To speak of Macroon, minister of France,
Or tell of Scarymucci's rise and fall.
Instead, once more our history must jump:
A bright new year hath dawn'd upon the land,   10
With new threats rising for the bold MacTrump—
Against his bold opponents, shall he stand?
If this quick tempo seemeth unforgiving,
Remember: 'twas far harder in the living.
                                                  [Exit Chorus.

Enter DOCTOR PINO ENOS.

ENOS Wouldst thou be cur'd of all infirmities?   15
Wouldst stand aright where others slouch and fade?
Wouldst be erect where other men are limp?
Wouldst be prepar'd for ev'rything and nothing?
Then, see the Enos doctor, that is me!
I'll give thee purple pills for potency,   20

I'll suck the bile from thee to give thee vigor,
I'll bleed thy body 'til thy snake is drain'd,
To make thy bones more strong and straight and stout!
The Enos doctor worketh miracles
For mighty men—and sometimes women, too!   25
E'en now, I wait upon my lord MacTrump,
Who sees the Enos doctor frequently
To guarantee his flag doth fly full mast.

Enter MACTRUMP *with various* ATTENDANTS.

MACTRUMP   Pray, make this speedy. I have not all day.
ENOS   Holla, sir. I'll examine you anon.   30
                         [Doctor Enos uses calipers to
                              measure MacTrump's belly.
A girth befitting such a paragon,
For as the stomach grows, so grows the myth—
Circumf'rence is the measure of the great,
Be they Magellan or Copernicus.
Not e'en our largest bygone president,   35
Lord Falstaft, was as great as you are, sir.
                    [Doctor Enos uses an ear trumpet
                         to listen to MacTrump's heart.
The tick and tock of clockwork excellence—
Your heart could build a border wall itself
And let Mexitlán pay the doctor's fee.
                    [Doctor Enos places his hand on
                         top of MacTrump's head.
A pate of pure perfection, by my troth—   40
The presidential brain far larger than
The simpler minds that whine and gripe and moan

For not possessing such a proud, thick skull.
Say, sir, how do you feel?

MacTRUMP   —Fine.

ENOS   —Fine, forsooth—
No fitter frame or fairer face we'll find!   45
I do pronounce you, sir, in perfect health—
A specimen of human flawlessness.
Alas, the leeches I administer'd
All died of grief, for thy cholesterol
Did fill their sucking bellies with delight!   50

MacTRUMP   Such was my expectation. [*Calling:*] Ho, McTweet!
[*To Enos:*] Thou mayst depart—tell all what thou
                                     hast seen.
Speak freely of my genes incredible,
Employing the word *very* many times.
[*Quietly:*] And if thou meetest Nurse Sildenafil,   55
I bid thee send her to me urgently.

                           [*Exit Doctor Enos.*

Now I shall tell the world how fit I am—
It is not boasting if 'tis true. [*Calling:*] McTweet!

                 Enter McTweet.

McTWEET   You holler'd for me?

MacTRUMP   —Give me thy report:
Who hath said naughty things of me today?   60

McTWEET   King Stephen, Madame Rowlinge, Lady Warwick—
These all were critical—

MacTRUMP   —Pray, block their access.
I would not grant them leave to read my words.

McTWEET   Done.

MacTRUMP	—Then post in a trice: "The doctor sayeth
	Ne'er has there been a man who doth enjoy 65
	Such health and wealth and nat'ral skin and hair."
	Be sure thou usest exclamation point
	And whole words form'd in letters capital.
	Add thou, as well, one of thy hashbrown bags.
McTWEET	A hashtag, sir?
MacTRUMP	—Whatever. Get thee hence. 70
McTWEET	Ere I depart, I've some few words for you.
MacTRUMP	A message from McTweet? This bodes not well.
	What wouldst thou say? I bid thee, be direct.
McTWEET	Two things: first, there hath been another shooting.
	Shall I send forth your thoughts and pray'rs, my
	liege? 75
MacTRUMP	Indeed, and make it heartfelt, or whatever.
McTWEET	It shall be done. Now to the second matter:
	It is a message from a Tempest Daniels,
	A woman who declares she knows you well.
	An actress, I have gather'd, of some note. 80
	[*Aside:*] Though not on any stage that I have seen,
	For I have content filters most robust.
MacTRUMP	Er, Tempest Daniels. Well, what is her missive?
McTWEET	She'd speak with thee anon.
MacTRUMP	—'Tis all?
McTWEET	—Indeed.
	Farewell. Your post I shall dispatch with care. 85
	[*Exit McTweet.*
MacTRUMP	[*to attendants:*] Be gone, I need a moment's privacy.
	[*Exeunt attendants.*
	O, shall my past return to work me woe?
	Cannot what's past be past since it hath pass'd?

It is no more! It cannot be again.
The past hath no place in the present time,   90
Nor in the future—past is past is past.
How, then, doth it e'er rear its gruesome head?
I see a thing I like and I do take it.
I see a thing I want and I do own it.
'Tis appetite and nothing more nor less,   95
An ordinary, healthy thirst for pleasure.
'Tis nature! Wherefore should it do me harm?
Though I am certain I did fool McTweet,
Of course I do remember Tempest Daniels—
Yea, well do I recall each inch of her,   100
For, like so many ladies, she desir'd
To know MacTrump most intimately. Ha!
She sigh'd for my attention and did groan
For mine embrace, like all the female hordes.
The hordes, the whores, 'tis all the same to me.   105
She pin'd for me and long'd for me like one
So deep in love she would, most likely, drown.
Then Tempest—nay, I'll call her only Horseface—
Display'd her colors true once we did part,
Demanding compensation for her silence.   110
How like a woman, quick to mete revenge
When summer's love turns to a wintry chill.
Past, it seems I must deal with thee again.

Enter MICHAEL LaCÖHEN.

LaCÖHEN   My lord! Long time, no seeing—bada bing!
             You got some problems you need fixing, sir?   115
MacTRUMP   Ah, Michael, just thy voice brings cool relief.

Remember Tempest Daniels?

LACÖHEN —Yea, I do—
I never met a pair that I forgot.

MACTRUMP Did we not pay her?

LACÖHEN —We did so indeed—
One hundred forty thousand ducats, sir.   120

MACTRUMP One hundred forty! Think'st thou I am rich?

LACÖHEN Nay, sir. I know it.

MACTRUMP —Never mind. It seems
She wanteth something more.

LACÖHEN —And more and more—
'Twas ever thus among unruly ladies.
Methinks 'tis wherefore it's call'd blackmail, sir—   125
The blackest hearts attack the blameless males.

MACTRUMP Canst fix it? Make it swiftly go away?
The check, as they do say, is in the mail.

LACÖHEN I'll see what I can do, sir. Bada boom!

[Exit LaCöhen.

MACTRUMP Beset on ev'ry side by enemies,   130
Now ladies, too, do turn their beaks on me.
Would that they all were kind as Desdivanka!
Yet nay, this Horseface and her broody kind
Are all the same, fowls looking for a cock.
If I am to be peck'd by ev'ry hen,   135
I'll need the Enos doctor once again.

[Exit.

SCENE 2.

Two months later.
A presidential palace in Helsingfort.

Enter MACTRUMP *and* JOURNALISTS *into a*
great hall. All walk with haste.

JOURNALIST 1   Please, Master President, I bid you, speak:
Is't true you tried to thwart the Deaf Beehive's
Investigation into Prussian meddling
When you abruptly sack'd Sir James Dogcomey?

MACTRUMP   A stupid question. Thou art stupid, too,   5
For ne'er have I obstructed anything!
There definitely hath been no obstruction.
Yet even if there were, my wise attorney
Doth counsel that obstruction is no crime.

JOURNALIST 2   You mean attorney Michael LaCöhen,   10
Whose home and offices were raided by
The Deaf Beehive last month?

MACTRUMP   —O, nay. Not him.
I mean my new attorney who comes hither.

                              [All gasp.

JOURNALIST 3   He's here? Great Fooliani?

MACTRUMP   —Even he.

Fanfare. Enter FOOLIANI *in a jester's costume*
bedecked with jingling bells.

FOOLIANI   [*to journalists:*] Take heed! All my complicit client

                                              says   15

                Is counterfactu'lly correct, indeed.

                There hath been no collusion rank betwixt

                The Prussian government and those key players

                In the MacTrump campaign. [*Aside:*] Yea, I should

                                              know,

                For I reviewèd each illegal act   20

                His campaign undertook! [*To journalists:*] The

                                       president

                Hath brought me here, this crisis to defuse,

                Ere it becomes a circus most diffuse.

                      [Fooliani shakes his marotte. Bells jingle.

MACTRUMP   [*to Fooliani:*] Canst thou respond to all these losers'

                                       queries?

                I fain would use the bathroom hastily.   25

FOOLIANI   [*to MacTrump:*] You shall not miss the door, I'll

                                    warrant, sir.

                I bang'd my giant head upon it now.

                        [Bells jingle. Exit MacTrump.

                [*To journalists:*] As I began to say to ye, my client

                Is innocent of charges of collusion,

                Conspiracy so to commit collusion,   30

                And other crimes we ne'er shall know about

                For he is innocent of them. In sooth,

                If he, my client, guilty were of aught,

                'Tis being innocent. If that's a crime,

                I'll lead the chorus chanting, "Lock him up!"   35

JOURNALIST 3   Great Fooliani, wherefore did MacTrump

                Call European allies losers since

                They owe th'United Fiefdoms heaps of money?

FOOLIANI	'Tis leadership! Is't not? Our nation spent
	A fortune keeping allies safe for decades. 40
	'Tis far past time they paid us for it! Ha!
JOURNALIST 1	Great Fooliani, doth the late indictment
	Of President MacTrump's campaign chair Paulus
	Romanafort, on charges of conspiracy,
	Involve aught that MacTrump will speak about 45
	In private with Putain this afternoon?
FOOLIANI	Dost thou have any notion of the number
	Of chairs in that campaign? 'Twas dozens. More!
	Shall we arrest the furniture because
	MacTrump the Junior innocently sat 50
	With Prussian envoys at a table meeting?
	If so, MacMueller peradventure would
	Be call'd t'arrest MacTrump's own rug as well!
JOURNALIST 3	Great Fooliani, what of the indictment
	Of Prussian military bureaucrats 55
	For filching Democrati messages?
FOOLIANI	If 'twere, in fact, illegal, Lord MacTrump
	Would not have ask'd the Prussian government
	To steal more of them during the campaign.
	He is no fool. 'Tis wherefore he hir'd me! 60
JOURNALIST 1	Dost thou, though, hold with President MacTrump's
	Own comments: that the Democrati Party
	Is fill'd with criminals of poor IQ?
FOOLIANI	Of course I do! How soon you folks forget
	That I was once a Democrato, too. 65

                 [Fooliani shakes his marotte. Bells jingle.

JOURNALIST 3	What of reports, ongoing, of the children
	Who, near our border, still are lock'd in cages?
FOOLIANI	I never met a child who did not love

To visit creatures in menageries.
Our southern compound where the children wait 70
Is but a trial full-immersion zoo.

JOURNALIST 3 Doth th'administration verily consider
The fam'lies concentrated in these camps
Part of a zoo?

FOOLIANI —Of course! There shall be such
Across the land, with many tickets sold. 75
They may make better profit than our prisons!

JOURNALIST 2 Why did MacTrump sack herald Spicero?

FOOLIANI Because he—Spicero—became a shrub
And like a tree he had to leaf anon.

Enter MacTRUMP *as a toilet is heard flushing.*

MacTRUMP [*aside to Fooliani:*] My God, 'twas brutal.

FOOLIANI [*aside to MacTrump:*] —Nay, 'twas leadership. 80

MacTRUMP It was. Great Fooliani, prithee show
These clowns the door on which thou struck'st thyself.

FOOLIANI I'll show them with mine own head. Follow me!
[*Fooliani exits, charging headfirst*
through the doors.

JOURNALIST 1 Yet, Master President, will you discuss
Aught of the bold MacMueller inquisition 85
Withal the Prussian czar this afternoon?

JOURNALIST 2 Will your interpreter be present there?

JOURNALIST 3 Why did you hire the jester Fooliani?

JOURNALIST 1 What is your comment, sir, about Flynnaldo,
Who recently hath giv'n a guilty plea 90
Because he lied unto the Deaf Beehive?

MacTRUMP You pesky peasants, I've no time for this!

I shall anon meet my most powerful
And vital ally in the world! Get hence!
> *[MacTrump shoos the journalists out*
> *the door. Exeunt journalists.*

O, I am sorely vex'd. My bowels feel   95
An 'twere a cannon factory in flames.
[*Calling:*] McTweet!

Enter McTweet.

McTWEET   —Methought I was the cuckoo
                                          here.

MacTRUMP   Be quiet, bird beak. Tell thy featherbrains . . .
> *[McTweet picks up his quill and starts writing.*

Full many calls from allies I've receiv'd,
All thanking me for bringing them together   100
To focus them upon the gold they owe.
It truly was a summit most superb,
Which was inaccurately cover'd by
Much of the media ringmasters false.
Our proud alliance is both strong and rich!   105
Old lord O'Bama thought Hillaria
Was bound to win th'election easily—
Thus, when the Deaf Beehive sought to pursue
The Prussian meddling, he did not allow't.
'Twas no big deal and he did naught about it.   110
When I prevail'd, a big deal it became,
Thus prompting the rigg'd Witch Hunt by Z'Strzok!

McTWEET   [*aside:*] Now witches have been added to the plot?
This play's American, not Scottish, yea?
Are we in Helsingfort or Salem now?   115

MacTRUMP	Relationship with Prussia ne'er was worse
	Than now 'tis, thanks to years of foolishness,
	Stupidity, and, now, the rigg'd Witch Hunt!
McTWEET	Shall that be ev'rything, my lord?
MacTRUMP	—Not yet.

MacTRUMP   How long until Putain arriveth here?   120

McTWEET   I know not, sir. The news reports that he
                     Should have arriv'd an hour ago at least.

MacTRUMP   O. Prithee, wilt thou stay until he comes?

*[McTweet sticks his quill in his
cap and leaps into a chair.*

McTWEET   I am on standby, Lord MacTrump!

MacTRUMP   —My thanks.

*[Time passes. A clock ticks noisily.
MacTrump looks about the room.*

             What kind of palace is this sad excuse?   125
             'Tis stark and empty. Where's the fancy swag?
             The bathroom fixtures, tubs, and golden showers?
             The sculptures and the prints of naked ladies?

McTWEET   Would you like me to ask your followers?

MacTRUMP   Nay. I'd not have them see me presently.   130

McTWEET   No pictures, then?

MacTRUMP   —Nay, absolutely none!

The main doors to the room open. Enter VLAD PUTAIN,
Czar of the Prussian Federation, and his INTERPRETER.

        [*To McTweet:*] Be gone.

McTWEET   —With fluttering of wings
                        and feathers.
                    [Exit McTweet.

MacTRUMP   How are you, Comrade Vlad? Your mien looks well!
            Did you get those MacTrump steaks I did send?
            They're from 2007. A good year!   135
                    [MacTrump extends a hand, but Putain
                    unbuttons his coat and sits. MacTrump
                    follows suit. Putain speaks in Prussian.

INTERPRETER The czar apologizeth heartily
            For causing you to wait so long, my lord.

MacTRUMP   [*to Putain:*] 'Tis nothing, by my troth. I was admiring
            The awe-inspiring artwork in this palace.
            A most fine palace 'tis. And very yuge.   140
            Would that we had such palaces within
            Our own United Fiefdoms. I once tried
            To build one in New Yorktown, but they would
            Not let me do so. Such a shame. I wanted—
                    [Putain speaks in Prussian.

INTERPRETER The czar doth share your fondness for fine art   145
            And architecture. He says that this hall
            Was fashion'd in the manner Romanesque.

MacTRUMP   [*to Putain:*] Is that what this is? I love Romanesque.
            'Tis certainly my favorite type of building.
                    [The interpreter translates. Putain
                    smiles and responds in Prussian.

INTERPRETER The president declares he was mistaken.   150
            He says this hall is in Gothic style,
            Which is why it is call'd Gothic Hall.
                    [MacTrump nods, rebuffed.

MacTRUMP   [*to Putain:*] We all make our mistakes. Yea, even you.
                    [The interpreter translates this. Putain's
                    smile disappears. He replies in Prussian.

INTERPRETER The president says 'twas a simple joke.

MacTRUMP   O. Is that what he meant? Well, ha! A-ha!   155
                       [MacTrump laughs uneasily.
         Ha-ha, ha, ha-ha! [*He clears his throat.*] Thanks,
                                I love a joke.
                     [Putain speaks in Prussian.

INTERPRETER   The czar desires to be upfront with you,
         My Lord MacTrump. Your troubl'd presidency
         Doth not proceed at all as we had plann'd.
         Your European allies have united   160
         Against your rule. Your popularity
         Is plummeting at home and overseas.
         Your frail administration is a wreck.
         And you, the czar is saddened to report,
         Are artful in the realm political   165
         As an orangutan with feces is.

MacTRUMP   [*to Putain:*] What, Vlad, did you expect? The people
                                    you
         Told me to fill my staff with prov'd but losers.
         That surgeon guy believes in unicorns.
         My education secretary thinks   170
         The first man on the moon was made of cheese.
         The Gargamiller nut is barely human.
         And O, that dumb Secessions character?
         You Prussians pick'd the wrong horse for your bet!
         Why did you recommend him at the start?   175
         Not only did we lose his Senate seat,
         But he did naught to stop MacMueller's work!
         'Tis nearly like you wanted me to fail.
                    [Putain and his interpreter discuss.

INTERPRETER   The president doth ask if you will need
         Assistance in preventing Democrati   180

Takeovers in your parliament and states.

MacTRUMP   [*to Putain:*] Methinks 'tis not a good idea just now.

Can you help me more slyly than before?

I cannot drain my lizard sans a lawsuit

O'er what I did some thirty years ago.   185

They stop at naught, e'en interviewing girlfriends,

Exploring business deals that I have made,

And placing half my campaign staff in jail.

The whole thing is a nightmare in th'extreme!

If you could cause Republicons to win   190

In each election, 'twould be marvelous.

Yet it must be believable, forsooth.

Believe me, I know how the maggots work.

'Tis like a good casino: you must make

It seem like any coxcomb hath a chance.   195

If not, the sorry circus of a show

Will finish belly-up—like my casinos.

            [Putain and his interpreter speak privately.

Please, sirs, include me in the conversation.

For all that glitters, I am President

Of the United Fiefdoms, verily—   200

Yea, the most pow'rful man in all the world.

O, can you understand? My visage will

Be someday printed on a dollar bill—

Some new denomination wondrous large—

The selfsame UF dollar Prussia can   205

But dream of having! Listen to me, Vlad,

I do not care how many videos

You have of me with double-crossing harlots.

If you desire your half of Europe back,

You need my help far more than I need you!   210

Be reasonable. I have suffer'd plenty!

[Putain speaks in Prussian.

INTERPRETER   The mighty czar declareth he believes
You know not suffering, and never will.

MacTRUMP   [*to Putain:*] Is this another of your Prussian jokes?
I have not suffer'd? Ha! My father gave me   215
A mere one million dollars to begin.
Do you not comprehend how meager 'tis?
Do you but realize how hard I did fight
To change that pittance to a global empire?

[Putain speaks in Prussian.

INTERPRETER   No lies, my Lord MacTrump. You did receive   220
More than four hundred million from your father,
And somehow squander'd ev'ry cent and more.

MacTRUMP   [*to Putain:*] Bah! One must money spend to money
make!

Bethink you of the many people I
Paid off! The doctors, lawyers, governors,   225
Thugs, plastic surgeons, builders, mistresses!
When I put on my face, it costs a fortune.
My hair? Nay, prithee, do not get me started.
I am surrounded constantly by those
Who owe me money, more who owe me favors,   230
Yet on the instant I make headlines for
Some innocent and meaningless mistake,
They happily would stuff me like a buck.
The people in the White Hold hate me so.
Nobody trusteth me, not e'en my wives.   235
They who do work for me despise my soul.
I have not mov'd my bowels in three days,
And I can barely sleep a wink at night.

If it appears to you I am not suff'ring,
Mayhap it is because I'm best at it!   240
I've suffer'd more than you shall ever know—
Yet if you are not careful, you may learn!
              [Silence. Putain nods to his interpreter, who
                    exits. Putain then rises from his chair.

PUTAIN   Dorogoy droog, attend: if I may say,
                I must respectf'lly disagree with thee.
                Thou dost not know what suff'ring is, MacTrump, 245
                For suffering is not made for the weak.
                Thou art misled, for suff'ring makes one stronger.
                To suffer is to be invaded by
                Germanic hordes, to see thy homeland sweet
                Turn to a battlefield for centuries.   250
                To suffer's to watch children starve to death
                Because of thy resolve to fight off foes.
                To suffer is to know thy country could
                Break any minute into warring states.
                To suffer's to see fam'lies torn apart   255
                Whilst children slowly waste away in cages,
                As they do now along thy southern border.
                To suffer is what separates the strong
                From those incapable of their survival.
                This is, then, why I fear thy Democrati   260
                Foes are more powerful than thou dost think;
                They've suffer'd more than thou and all thy droogs.
                Thou wilt ne'er suffer quite as much as they;
                Thy country simply doth not work that way.

MacTRUMP   Pray, do not worry o'er those losers, Vlad.   265
                You have, I'll warrant, no idea how hard
                It is for them to even vote right now.

Our voter fraud campaign? 'Tis beautiful.
The troll who's making changes to the census
Shall buy us ten more years in charge at least. 270
MacTuttle, Pubis, and our governors
Are working to make Democrati votes
Far harder to be plac'd than e'er before.
'Tis passing yuge. You'll not believe your eyes
'Tis something like a last stand, by my troth. 275
And if we win this battle, we shall be
In charge of ev'rything we e'er could want.

PUTAIN Except MacMueller's inquisition, da?

MacTRUMP Yet in my country, Vlad, it matters not
Exactly how one wins at anything. 280
'Tis all a spectacle, a fantasy.
All that doth matter is that one doth win.
If one but wins, 'tis only the beginning.

[Putain rises.

PUTAIN Then win.

MacTRUMP —We shall. There shall be so much winning.

[Exeunt.

SCENE 3.

*Senator MacTuttle's suite in the Northern
Chamber of Parliament.*

Enter SENATOR MITCH MacTUTTLE, *playing a solitary
game of cards behind his desk. Enter his* SECRETARY.

SECRETARY	Forgive th'intrusion, Senator MacTuttle—
	The Democrati leaders have arriv'd.
MacTUTTLE	My thanks. I pray, remove the furniture.

[The secretary bows and begins removing all
the chairs from MacTuttle's office, save the
senator's. The last item removed is a long sofa,
which the secretary shoves out the door.

SECRETARY	Will that be all, sir?
MacTUTTLE	—Yea. Please send them in.

[Exit secretary. MacTuttle collects
his cards and pockets them.

Enter LADY NANCY PROSPEROSI
and SENATOR CHARLES SOOTHER.

SOOTHER	Good afternoon, fair Senator MacTuttle.	5

[MacTuttle rises.

MacTUTTLE	[*to Soother:*] Minor'ty Leader. [*To Prosperosi:*]
	Ma'am.
PROSPEROSI	[*correcting:*] —'Tis Madam Leader.
MacTUTTLE	Of course. [*Smiling:*] I bid you, sit ye down awhile.

[MacTuttle sits as Prosperosi and
Soother look around the office.

SOOTHER	Kind colleague, I can see no chairs for us.
MacTUTTLE	That is correct. [*Smiling:*] Please sit. You have the
	floor.

[Soother appears surprised;
Prosperosi is insulted.

PROSPEROSI	Sir, dost thou know that in the full eight years	10
	Your Democrati predecessor held	
	Thine office, he ne'er show'd thee e'en an ounce	

	Of this vile insult thou hast shown just now?
MacTUTTLE	My Democrati predecessor, Reid,
	Ne'er held an office such as is mine own, 15
	And I thank God above he never did.
	Yet if thy former leader ran things as
	I do, he might have more successful been.
SOOTHER	Of course—vast health care laws, an energiz'd
	Economy, and num'rous victories 20
	That thou and all thy powers fail'd to thwart—
MacTUTTLE	And two more High Court justice seats: a feat
	I shall achieve in half the time as he.
PROSPEROSI	I see no reason, sir, for thee to boast
	O'er aught that was obtain'd through thievery. 25
MacTUTTLE	Ma'am, I know thou know'st there's no such thing as
	A union perfect. We've had numerous
	Past presidents claim power through such means.
	To hold oneself unto decorum for
	The sake of that decorum is but folly. 30
	I did exploit an opportunity
	Provided by the way our system functions.
	Thou shouldst adore such brazen patriotism.
PROSPEROSI	I should abhor such brazen patronizing!
MacTUTTLE	O, patronizing? [*To Soother:*] This is why you
	came— 35
	But to insult me in the guise of peace?
SOOTHER	My colleague, surely know'st thou 'tis not so.
	We've hither come to gauge if compromise
	Is possible with thee and Congress both.
	Our system hath been built on compromises 40
	No differently than bicycles are built
	With wheels of two. No bike whose wheels do spin

In opposite directions calls itself
A bicycle for long—we need our system
To roll if we would keep MacTrump in check.   45
Thy party made a bargain with the devil
A long time past, which—as Faust learn'd—is hellish.
Thou canst not, by thyself, control MacTrump.
To tie the devil to a pillow takes
Two hands. If he's not tied, all hell breaks loose.   50

MacTUTTLE   Methinks not, Master Soother. Compromise
Hath always been a hindrance in this country.
Wars are not won through compromise, but by
Completely crushing all one's enemies.

SOOTHER   We are not enemies. We're friends.

MacTUTTLE   —We're not.   55
Why dost thou think we fought a civil war
With one another in the days of yore?
'Twas not a compromise; 'twas warfare bleak.
The South has not forgotten our just cause
Of southern rights to peace and property.   60

PROSPEROSI   And slavery.

MacTUTTLE   —Nay, and supremacy.
The party of Republicons that beat
The South hath fallen firmly in our hands.
Now we're the party that hath won the war.
As long as I shall stand as Senate leader,   65
The Democrati are our enemies.

PROSPEROSI   Thou hast no power constitutional
To exercise thy power in that manner.
Thine office does not e'en exist within
The Constitution!

MacTUTTLE   —Yet whose fault is that?   70

             Recall that neither of you did complain
             About my duties when someone among
             Your Democrati leaders held them. True?
             Thus, when O'Bama came to power, what
             Compulsion did we have to work with him?   75
             I did what I felt best t'advance mine own.
             O'Bama was a rank affront to millions
             Of people in this country. All I did
             Was guarantee their chosen senators
             Would fight against his rule with all our might.   80

PROSPEROSI   They did fight. It was callèd an election.
             The Democrati won.

MacTUTTLE   —Yet not for long.

SOOTHER   Thou didst not fairly fight, my colleague dear.
             Thou hast abusèd ev'ry pow'r we had,
             With which the Constitution would protect   85
             The party that is in minority.

MacTUTTLE   Is there a law against minorities
             Aspiring to become majorities?
             You're both in the minority today,
             Just as I was. If you cannot escape it,   90
             Belike 'tis there that you belong.

PROSPEROSI   —Fie on't!
             My whole life long I've suffer'd men like thee,
             Complaining over despotism foul,
             And tyranny as well, when thou'rt in power.
             Thy kind exploit each prejudice and fear   95
             To whitewash the reality of truth:
             That thy best years are gone, and thou hast lost!
             This too: America hath ever been
             More powerful in its diversity

	Than it e'er could be under white male rule.	100
MAcTUTTLE	Thou hast been warn'd, with explanation giv'n:	
	Yet nevertheless thou persisted still.	
	Rude woman, thou art standing in the office	
	Of the most pow'rful person in the country.	
	I do control the fate of all three branches	105
	Of government. I hold the power to	
	Decide what justice is for generations.	
	I am not bounded by term limits, nay,	
	And I come from a state that would select	
	A warthog to elected office if	110
	The animal were but Republicon.	
	I have denied them health, yet they support me.	
	I have denied them jobs, yet they support me.	
	I have denied them schools, food, better housing,	
	A safe environment, yet they support me.	115
	Why? 'Tis because I do belong in pow'r,	
	Be it by some divine and holy right	
	Or merely strength of mine own solid will.	
	Think on it: ev'ryone who held my office	
	Was white and male, and ev'ryone who held	120
	Thy colleague Soother's office? White and male.	
	Thou art the lone exception—aberration—	
	In some two hundred years of history.	
	'Tis not impressive, nay. 'Tis merely a	
	Statistical anomaly that shall	125
	Be easily corrected by white men	
	And by white women, too, throughout the country.	
	Such is our land, and I stand proud therein.	
	If thou dost like it not, I bid thee leave.	
	Thou'rt not a necessary part of it.	130

SOOTHER   For how much longer, my dear senator,
Dost thou believe MacTrump will think thou art
A necessary part of his regime?

MacTUTTLE   Naught hath been writ within the Constitution
With which MacTrump can threaten me, and he   135
Cannot invent one sans mine own approval,
Which shall, I need not say, ne'er come to pass.
And should he threaten me in any way,
I'll execute my constitutional
Responsibility by calling for   140
The vote for his removal from high office,
So that a wiser, less disruptive, and
Far weaker man nam'd Pound can take his place.

PROSPEROSI   Thou hast forgot there are two chambers in
Our Congress, Master Senator, and that   145
Impeachment starts inside the Southern wing.

MacTUTTLE   'Tis true, and much good luck to thee in setting
That house in order. 'Tis a woman's job,
Yet thou wert ne'er the woman for the task.
Mayhap that hammer was too heavy for   150
Thy Democrati sensibilities.

PROSPEROSI   Far better is a woman for the job
Than spineless boys too tiny for tall tasks.

MacTUTTLE   'Tis certain Speaker Pryam's a disaster,
Yet I'd take ten of him to one of thee.   155

SOOTHER   For such a man of power, Senator,
Thou dost surround thyself with feeble allies.

MacTUTTLE   So speaks the leader of minorities.
Excuse me, but the time I have for ye
Is all elaps'd. Go hence about your business.   160

PROSPEROSI   Enjoy thy pride before thou fall'st, MacTuttle!

MacTUTTLE   A first-rate fall I do anticipate,
                   Good Lady Prosperosi. I wish thee
                   And thy friends fortune in our next election.

                   [Exeunt Prosperosi and Soother. MacTuttle
                   returns to his playing cards and smiles.

Enter SECRETARY.

SECRETARY   Master MacTuttle, Viceroy Michael Pound   165
                   Is here for you.

MacTUTTLE   —Our meeting may commence.

Enter VICEROY MICHAEL POUND,
Viceroy of the United Fiefdoms.

MacTUTTLE   'Tis well to see you, Mike.

POUND   —Your Eminence!

                   [MacTuttle offers Pound his hand. The
                   viceroy delightfully kisses it. Exeunt.

SCENE 4.

In the White Hold and the Oval Tower.

Enter LADY SARAH PUCKABEE *above, on*
balcony, with several JOURNALISTS.

PUCKABEE   Be seated, gentles.

[The journalists sit.
—Are there any questions?
[The journalists break into a rabble.
One question at a time, I prithee, hens!

JOURNALIST 1   Why did MacTrump and Putain speak alone,
Sans even an interpreter therein?

PUCKABEE   That story's categorically false.   5
For how could anyone see them alone
Unless they, too, were somehow in the room?

JOURNALIST 2   What doth MacTrump think of MacMueller's latest?
Now that Romanafort is gone, who's next?

PUCKABEE   The president was never a mind reader.   10
Lord Gargamiller is; go thou ask him.

JOURNALIST 3   Shall President MacTrump still build his wall,
E'en if Americans do want it not?

PUCKABEE   If President MacTrump says he will build
A wall, then he shall do so whether all   15
His faithless peasants wish him to or not.

JOURNALIST 4   Say, wherefore is it that Lady MacTrump
Hath not been seen these recent weeks in public?

PUCKABEE   Lady MacTrump is fine, yet occupied.
It, also, is offensive in the height—   20
Thine implication that Lady MacTrump
Doth need to be in public at all times
To be of service as a public figure!

JOURNALIST 2   What of the border cages—

PUCKABEE   —Not again,
Unless thou wouldst go babysit the brats!   25

JOURNALIST 1   And what of Spicero?

PUCKABEE   —We still do search
Each bush and shrub in Washingtown for him.

[The journalists begin talking among themselves.
Pray, be ye still, purveyors of fake news!
I am the newfound herald of MacTrump,
And shall respond to all your questions when   30
I have the means, the time, and the desire.
    [Exeunt Puckabee with journalists, in confusion.

            Enter MacTRUMP.

MacTRUMP   The freedom of the press doth press me hard,
                Indeed, it hath me up against a wall
                (And not the border wall for which I long,
                Which I do dangle over my supporters   35
                Like they were asses and the wall the carrot).
                The press, the journalists, the rank fake news
                Surround me like a pack of rabid dogs
                Who'd gladly bite me with their rancid teeth.
                They know no reason and spread only lies.   40
                Mayhap there's one, though, who would hear some
                                                        sense:
                The newsman fam'd who brought down Richard
                                                        th'Worst,
                E'en Robert Wormwood. [*Calling:*] Hither,
                                                        Kelleyanne!

            Enter LADY KELLEYANNE BOLEYN.

KELLEYANNE   Yes, liege? You call'd and I have come anon,
                Plus-eager to please you than mine own husband.   45
MacTRUMP   I prithee summon Robert Wormwood here,
                I need the journalist to speak with me.

KELLEYANNE   At once. Pray, wait a moment—he shall come.

                               [Exit Kelleyanne.

             Enter ROBERT WORMWOOD.

MACTRUMP   Ho, Robert.

WORMWOOD   —President MacTrump, good day.

            With your permission, I'll record this meeting.   50

                  [Wormwood pulls out a quill

                         as if to begin writing.

MACTRUMP   [*aside:*] Of course thou shalt, thou wicked, rotting

                                  rat—

            Recorders are the shields of craven newsmen.

            [*To Wormwood:*] 'Tis well, I do not mind, not in the

                                 least.

WORMWOOD   You've summon'd me, I'll wager, o'er my book.

MACTRUMP   [*aside:*] A book? What is this book of which you

                              speak?   55

            Methinks I wrote a book once, did I not?

            I know words, yea—I have the best of words.

            [*To Wormwood:*] Just now I spake with Kelleyanne,

                                and she

            Knows naught of any book—didst thou not call?

            Whom didst thou ask about a talk with me?   60

WORMWOOD   Near six of your own staff.

MACTRUMP   —They told me not.

WORMWOOD   A senator as well. 'Twas two months since

            I first ask'd Kelleyanne if I could speak

            With you about this book. Apologies,

            The book must forward move without your input.   65

MACTRUMP   Must it? O Robert, thou wert ever fair.

WORMWOOD   [*aside:*] From fair to fear in one blink of the eye.
               [*To MacTrump:*] If you would speak again before
                                                    the book
               Hath its release into the public eye,
               You know full well how you may reach me, sir.   70
MACTRUMP   But Robert, I am so afeard these days—
               MacMueller cometh for my very life!
               Thou hast forever work'd in Washingtown—
               Canst not give me a morsel of advice?
WORMWOOD   'Tis not my place, nay. I bid you farewell.   75
                                        [*Exit Wormwood.*
MACTRUMP   Alack, no help or succor he provides!
               [*Hailing:*] McTweet, I bid thee come again.

                       Enter MCTWEET.

McTWEET   —You sang?
MACTRUMP   First, thou must post some messages for me.
McTWEET   Mayhap you'd like count to ten first, sir?
MACTRUMP   Nay, prithee send this missive sans delay: 80
               "If 'twas the goal of Prussia to create
               Discord and chaos and disruption in
               Our great United Fiefdoms then, with all
               The hearings, inquisitions base and vile,
               And party hatred, they succeed beyond   85
               Their wildest dreams, and laugh like asses rare
               In Moskvá. Be ye smart, America!"
McTWEET   [*aside:*] 'Twas well my char'cter limit doubl'd lately.
               [*To MacTrump:*] 'Tis done. Is there aught else, your
                                                    tweetfulness?
MACTRUMP   Next, I'd vouchsafe to thee a secret word,   90

                    Sans which a person may not further pass.

McTWEET   You'd have me change your password?

MACTRUMP   —Right thou art.

                    Canst thou be trusted with a thing as this?

McTWEET   If you desire, I'll share my terms of service:

                    "These terms of service govern access to   95

                    And use of all our services, including

                    Our various web platforms, SMS,

                    Our buttons, widgets, ads, and APIs,

                    Our email notices, our applications,

                    And other cover'd services as well—"   100

MACTRUMP   Already dost thy prattling ache my head.

                    I know you may be trusted, else I would

                    Not call on thee when I have need of thee.

                    Art thou prepar'd to take the password?

McTWEET   —Yea.

MACTRUMP   It is *covfefe.*

McTWEET   —Co-thief?

MACTRUMP   —Covfefe! Art deaf?   105

McTWEET   I see: two Fs, one V, one O, two Es,

                    As in the saying "thirty-five to life."

MACTRUMP   Thou impudent—

McTWEET   —It hath been chang'd, my lord.

                                [Exit McTweet.

MACTRUMP   When e'en the messengers show disrespect,

                    A ruler's in a sad and lonely place—   110

                    Worse than the woods wherein Hillaria hides.

                    Aught need I that shall spark a better mood.

                    Regrettably, affairs are frown'd upon

                    Within the confines of the Oval Tow'r—

                    Not that it stopp'd O'Clinton with Moninski.   115

What else shall make me glad? I would eat more,
Yet have just fill'd my gullet with a meal
That could have fed a hundred hungry wretched souls
Who beg on Pennsylvanus Avenue.
If not mine appetite for fubbing off,   120
Nor my quotidian delight in food,
What shall it be? A-ha! The thought doth come:
I'll call upon my loving family
To have them say such pleasant things of me
That I shall find my humor once again.   125
Whilst they are here, I shall make certain to
Give them the password spoken to McTweet.
[*Calling:*] What ho, sweet Desdivanka, wilt thou
                                            come?
Pray Donnison and Ericson, come, too!

Enter DAME DESDIVANKA, DONNISON, *and* ERICSON.

DESDIVANKA   My noble father!
                              [She kisses MacTrump.
DONNISON   —Lord MacTrump.
ERICSON   —Ho, Dad!   130
MacTRUMP   My loving children, come to bring me joy:
              Which of you shall we say doth love us most?
ERICSON   I love you more than words can wield the matter.
              There is no wide savanna on the earth
              That can contain the words that would express   135
              My boundless, deep affection for my liege.
DONNISON   My brother comes too short. My love is such
              That, were your enemies to harp on you,
              Delivering foul blights upon your name,

I'd gladly snap their cords with mine own hands.   140

DESDIVANKA My brothers miss the mark; they are in error,
And love you far too little than your worth.
For if I ever doubted you myself,
I'd cut mine own heart out ere I'd betray you.

MacTRUMP Yet mayhap I am not so very great?   145
How can ye three assure me I am great?

ERICSON Among the presidents you are the best.

DONNISON Among Americans you are the best.

DESDIVANKA Among humanity you are the best,
Surpassing all the fathers ever known—   150
Dealmaker, businessman, negotiator,
Disruptor of the fusty status quo,
The wooer of a thousand ladies' hearts,
Tycoon and self-made billionaire as well,
Now leader of the planet's strongest nation.   155

MacTRUMP O, more delightful children there were ne'er.
How do you fare? What is the latest news?

DONNISON Dear Father, Ericson and I are sad
Because we have not found the love we seek.
'Twas many months ago we saw two ladies   160
Who sent us missives that would make you blush,
Yet when we went to the appointed place
Where we should meet them, only we were there—
The two of us, each looking for a love,
Yet finding only one another. Fie!   165

ERICSON Since then, we each have sent more messages
And question'd why the ladies left us so,
Yet they respond as if they too were there
And think that we abandon'd them. O, Father!
Is not love hard?

MacTRUMP	—I find it somewhat limp. 170
	Yet you two have my sympathy, my boys.
	Methinks such men will find what they do seek,
	Though why you seek to earn a lady's love
	Is aught that I may never understand,
	For I have ever found them fickle things. 175
DONNISON	But tender.
ERICSON	—Soft.
DONNISON	—And luscious.
MacTRUMP	—Silly fools.
	[*To Desdivanka:*] What of thee, daughter? What
	plays on thy mind?
DESDIVANKA	Good Father, rather than become a bore
	With matters of the state wherein I move,
	Let us proceed to more important topics. 180
	You call'd us here for some great purpose, yea?
MacTRUMP	I have. Sweet children, produce of my loins,
	The longer I do serve as president—
	Indeed, the greater grows mine own life's span—
	The more I see the need for family. 185
	My Democrati enemies are rank,
	Deceitful, petty, fill'd with ev'ry vice—
	Yet they, at least, are true unto their nature.
	'Tis the Republicons who disappoint
	By being weak and argumentative, 190
	When they should be the ones supporting me—
	They should be nearly falling o'er themselves
	To put MacTrump's agenda into action.
	Instead, they have profound mistrust for me,
	Believing ev'ry rotten thing they hear 195
	And ready to dissemble giv'n the chance.

E'en mine own staff considers me a burden,
Sir John MacKeeley—mine own aide-de-camp—
Abruptly questioning mine ev'ry move.
Dim Spicero, my herald to the public,   200
Did fumble each new sentence that he utter'd.
In times as these, my daughter and my sons,
I see 'tis only ye whom I can trust.
For I shall not be president fore'er—

DONNISON   Alack, say not so!

ERICSON   —Four more years!

DONNISON   —Nay, forty!   205

MᴀᴄTRUMP   Take heed: one day the world shall move along
And poor MacTrump will have to take a seat.
However—you who know me best can guess—
I'll not go gentle into that good night,
But rage against the dying of the light.   210
'Tis ye three who shall carry on my flame:
I'll pass the torch unto the next MacTrump
Who'll lead the masses onward to our glory.

DESDIVANKA   [*aside:*] This is the moment I must make my claim.
[*To MacTrump:*] Who, Father, shall it be? Which
                               child of yours? 215
Mine elder brother Donnison, a man
Both virtuous and most intelligent?
Or he, the younger, Ericson, who is
Courageous, strong, and agile as a wolf?
                [*Donnison and Ericson look
                   expectantly at MacTrump.*

MᴀᴄTRUMP   The boys are each a stately testament   220
Unto the fam'd MacTrump virility,
Yet neither is my choice to bear my mantle.

[Donnison and Ericson begin to protest.
Nay, Donnison and Ericson, be still:
Your sister Desdivanka hath a rare
Astounding, enviable set of skills.   225
Her cunning doth surpass the generals,
Her wisdom is beyond our top advisors,
Her strategies could best a host of foes,
And O, her beauty is without compeer.
She hath a pleasing figure, by my troth—   230
If she were not my daughter, mark my words:
Belike we two would soon be paramours.

DESDIVANKA   My liege, your words fall unexpectedly
Upon my grateful and most humble ears.
Your trust in me shall never be forsaken.   235

DONNISON   Though I stand 'fore you as the eldest son,
I do respect and will obey your verdict.
You, Father, are the finest judge of men—
And ladies, in this case.

ERICSON   —So shall I, too,
Be guided by your brighter, shrewder light.   240

MacTRUMP   Then 'tis decided. When I pass the reins—
In four or eight or sixteen years perchance—
'Twill be to Desdivanka, my delight.

[All embrace.
Meanwhile, I must give ye a pow'rful word,
Which shall unlock the powers of McTweet   245
And be a sign for those whose hearts are true—
I bid you, share this word with no one else
Outside the noble, potent House MacTrump.

DONNISON   We stand prepar'd and swear to God.

DESDIVANKA   *[to MacTrump:]*   —To you.

MacTRUMP	The word's *covfefe*.
DONNISON	—Covfefe?
ERICSON	—Covfefe!
DESDIVANKA	[*aside:*] —Good grief. 250
MacTRUMP	Come with me, children, dine with me anon;
	I feel another hunger coming on.

> [*Exeunt MacTrump, Donnison,*
> *and Ericson, embracing.*

DESDIVANKA Is this indeed the stock whence I have come,
A giant teat and his two suckling pigs?
Had I known Father's reign would be   255
So ruinous, I would have ask'd he make
Me viceroy moments after he took office.
Am I to be surrounded e'er by fools,
Behaving like mischievous brats, not men?
For now, I must be patient, and accept   260
That history moves slower than I wish.
I must keep ever closer to my father
And stay within his graces as the fav'rite,
Continuing to prove my worth, my wisdom,
And—since it pleaseth him—my beauty, too,   265
Enduring kisses and his hearty hugs.
My brothers I shall show a sister's smile,
Exaggerating all their dull achievements—
However few they are—and helping them
To navigate their silly lovesick hearts.   270
If I would wield, one day, the utmost pow'rs,
My part I must perform these final hours.

> [*Exit.*

SCENE 5.

*On the White Hold balcony,
and on the green below.*

Enter MacTRUMP, LADY MacTRUMP,
DAME DESDIVANKA, LORD JARED KUSHREW, DONNISON,
and ERICSON *above, on balcony.*

LADY M.	[*aside:*] The sun shall darken and our light shall dim,
	So say the clerics scientifical.
	Today, our blue orb shall eclipse the sun—
	What meaneth this strange omen for our lives?
	Shall my cold husband have his hopes eclips'd? 5
	Shall Democrati knaves eclipse his pow'r?
	Shall me and my sweet children be eclips'd?
	Will darkness cover o'er us like a shroud?
	Alack, methinks this is a dreadful portent,
	An evil demon come to work us woe. 10
	It is a pox, I say. A shiny pox!
	How can all those around me be so calm
	When ev'ry sign announces our defeat—
	Our horrid fall into the darkness drear?
	How can they laugh, in nondesigner eyewear, 15
	When all around us gloomy dusk doth loom?
	I must away, and hide myself anon,
	E'er our sun dies before my very eyes,
	A sight that I would never wish to see.
	Help, someone, help! The sun is falling! Help! 20

[Exit Lady MacTrump, sobbing and
unnoticed, into the White Hold.

MacTRUMP 'Tis certain that the realm entire doth wait
Upon this glorious event today.
A clear, good omen for my presidency,
An 'twere the heavens shouted all at once,
"MacTrump hath our approval in the heights!" 25
See how the people crowd around below,
Each straining to behold the lustrous sight.
Would that I were as popular as this—
A simple shadow blocking out a star.
Yet do I not shine brighter than the sun? 30
It is celestial, but I'm MacTrump!
I could take hold of it and make it mine—
Not fall like Icarus, the stupid chump.

Enter, on the green below, FOOLIANI *surrounded*
by JOURNALISTS. *Enter several* PROTESTORS *aside,*
including JUSTINE *and* MARIANNE.

JOURNALIST 1 [*to Fooliani:*] Excuse me, didst thou say the
president
Himself takes credit for the sun's eclipse? 35
FOOLIANI Nay, merely I said it cannot be prov'n
That President MacTrump hath not design'd
This wonderful event by his own pow'r.
JOURNALIST 2 Cannot be proven?
FOOLIANI —Prithee, show thy proof!
[Fooliani shakes his marotte. Bells jingle.
JOURNALIST 2 Nay, I have none. And yet—
FOOLIANI —My point is shown! 40

	The great MacTrump is so amazing that
	The sun itself doth hide within his presence.
	Behold him there, upon the balcony—
	Our true and wondrous leader proudly stands!
MacTRUMP	[*aside:*] I need to urinate, yet I must wait 45
	Until this silly pageant is complete.
DESDIVANKA	Good Father, what make you of this event?
MacTRUMP	Methinks it doth portend our great success.

        [He begins staring at the sun.

DESDIVANKA	'Tis my belief as well, my liege. And yet
	You should not stare directly on the sun. 50
MacTRUMP	They say it dims.
DESDIVANKA	—Yet 'tis still passing bright.
MacTRUMP	It darkens.
DESDIVANKA	—It shall roast your eyeballs, sir.

    [She hands him sunglasses, which he puts on
    reluctantly. Lord Kushrew approaches them.

MacTRUMP	[*to Kushrew:*] What thinkest thou, Lord Kushrew?
KUSHREW	—All is
	bright—
	The future shineth, full of expectation.
	[*To Desdivanka:*] Art thou most sure I cannot look
	on it? 55
DESDIVANKA	[*aside:*] My husband is as bad as mine own father—
	Are they but children, whom I must watch o'er?
	[*To Kushrew:*] Pray, wear these, Jared.
KUSHREW	—If thou dost
	insist.

    [All stare at the sky wearing sunglasses,
    except for Justine below on the green.

| JUSTINE | Pray, tell me what thou seest, Marianne. |

MARIANNE	My friend, today thou hast my sympathy. 60
	Yet since thou cannot see, hear thou these words,
	Writ by another bard: "We stand bemus'd . . .
	Until the sun and moon slide out of phase
	And light returns us to the common life
	That is so long to do and so soon done." 65
JUSTINE	'Tis beautiful. My thanks, dear sister mine.
	But there's no need for tears, for what I see
	With mine own mind is equally divine—
	Should one see stars as merely overhead,
	One lacks the sight to them perceive in full. 70
MARIANNE	I pray, my sister, what dost see? Do tell!
JUSTINE	I hear the sights and sounds of bated breaths,
	Of ev'ry man and woman, barking dogs
	And tweeting birds, each buzzing bee awake
	With utter wonder and confusion o'er 75
	The paranormal pull that lifts their pulse.
	I feel the gentle vapor of the river
	So cool against my skin in growing shade.
	I see each eye and soul around me turn'd
	Unto the sky, at the empyrean star 80
	That serves as mother to us all! And as
	She doth allow herself this precious moment
	To slip behind her silken screen, I see
	The suns and spheres all glowing ever brighter
	Than we have ever witness'd in the day. 85
	I see their paths and spins and pirouettes,
	I see their grand ballet: the Milky Way!
	O, dear companion, weep thou not for me,
	For such is the spectacular display
	Each person who doth share mine eyes' condition 90

                    Beholds on this exquisite, dimming day.

MARIANNE   Again, my sister, thou hast made me feel
                    As if I am the one who's truly blind!
                    I thank thee for thine insight. Now, tell me,
                    What dost thou think th'eclipse of solar light   95
                    Doth presage for our weary, troubl'd nation?

JUSTINE   Why ask'st thou this, my sister? Dost thou think
                    Our fates are written in the stars above?

MARIANNE   Of course! The heavens made us, verily.
                    Much have I ponder'd on this very question,   100
                    And this have I concluded: is it not
                    With some relief that we see this eclipse?
                    There are more things in heav'n and earth, Justine,
                    Than are dreamt of in our philosophy.
                    This day remindeth us that stronger forces   105
                    Exist than we shall ever comprehend.
                    No matter how much life doth overwhelm,
                    The planets move, the stars do rise and set.

JUSTINE   'Tis true. Yet while the heavens and the earth—
                    The universe's full expansiveness—   110
                    Do move in courses well beyond our ken,
                    Our planet, still, doth face a mighty threat—
                    A menace that could rend the earth in twain.

MARIANNE   The villain standing on his balcony.

JUSTINE   Indeed.

MARIANNE   —We must, then, ev'ry effort make   115
                    To stand against this threat while we have breath.
                    I would not see our liberty denied,
                    Nor watch as justice wholly is destroy'd.
                    Let us, then, promise by this dying light,
                    We two shall doggedly continue on   120

	To protest, yell, demand, provoke, resist,
	Until a truer light o'er us doth shine!
JUSTINE	Unto this cause I swear.
MARIANNE	—I swear as well,
	To thee and to th'America I love.

> [The light changes as totality arrives. All above
> and below stand silently, in awe. Slowly, the
> crowd below disperses until all exeunt.

MacTRUMP	'Tis over, at long last. And now, 'tis time	125
	To lift the leg and hose the porcelain.	

> [Exeunt MacTrump, Desdivanka, and Kushrew.

DONNISON	[to Ericson:] Ho, brother, thou shalt not believe	
	thine ears—	
	Methought I saw our ladies two below!	
ERICSON	Where, when?	
DONNISON	—Upon the White Hold green, just now.	
	Yet now the crowd is gone, and love withal.	130
ERICSON	Alas! I could not see them. Donnison?	
DONNISON	What?	
ERICSON	—I'm afeard.	
DONNISON	—Of this celestial portent?	
ERICSON	Nay, nay, I am afraid I may have look'd	
	Too long upon the sun and all its rays!	
DONNISON	Why think'st thou so? Pray, brother, canst thou see?	135
ERICSON	'Tis only multicolor'd spots I see,	
	Which take the shape of hearts before mine eyes.	
DONNISON	O, lovesick boy, I also saw those hearts—	
	In their sweet faces, talking on the green.	
ERICSON	You saw them, too?	
DONNISON	—Yea!	
ERICSON	—Wonders!	

DONNISON   —Let's inside; 140
          I'll warrant thou wilt see aright again.
          Pray, come inside and rest thy weary bones.
ERICSON   Once I am well, let us watch Dame of Thrones!
                              [Exeunt into the White Hold.

SCENE 6.

That night at the White Hold residence.

A toilet flushes. Enter MacTrump *in a presidential bathrobe.*

MacTRUMP   I am so troubl'd by the damn'd reporters
          Who question me o'er Prussians and MacMueller,
          My bow'ls do even mount their own resistance.
          The losers do not care how I may feel,
          Yet still am I in charge and run the show.   5
          My mind is plagu'd by constant overuse—
          One night of steady sleep is all I seek,
          To heal my weary, overburden'd mind.
          I had my nightly flagon of warm milk,
          My faithful stuffèd bear is here beside me,   10
          And mine attendants tuck'd me in with care—
          There's naught that can disturb this restful night.
                    [He climbs into bed and turns off the lights.

          Enter Ghost of Banquo O'Bama.

[MacTrump sits up in shock.

O'Bama's ghost! However can this be?
My senses may by many tricks be sway'd.
Belike my stomach maketh my mind weak—   15
You are, mayhap, some undigested beef,
Yet far more gravy than come from the grave.
Why are you here? Methought you had gone hence
To live in your post-presidential glow—
Yet somehow now old presidents return?   20
How are you hither come to wreak your—wait . . .
Why do you have a ghost? You're still alive.

O'BAMA   Because hope never dies.

Enter JOSEPH O'BIDEN.

O'BIDEN   —'Tis certain, Banqy!
O'BAMA   How art thou, Joe?
O'BIDEN   —Well. I receiv'd thy text.
MacTRUMP   O'Biden? Wait—thou art not e'en a ghost.   25
Who let thee in the White Hold?
O'BIDEN   —I know much
About this castle you could never grasp,
Like how to show respect unto your office
And work constructively with one's opponents—
The little things that make one great—again.   30
MacTRUMP   Pray listen, Joe, if thou wouldst harshly speak,
Then challenge me in 2020, rogue.
Thy visage mak'st me not afeard.
O'BIDEN   —Malarkey!
You quake with fear at facing me, MacTrump.
MacTRUMP   All right, I do. I shall confess it, yet   35

	That doth not make clear why the two of you
	Have hither come whilst I attempt to sleep.
O'BIDEN	I prithee, Banqy, explicate the matter.
O'BAMA	We've come to tell you that today's eclipse
	Foreshadows utter failure for your reign. 40
	You think yourself as mighty as the sun,
	Yet forces far beyond your influence
	Are coming to reduce your orange glow.
	Each one of us believeth we will be
	The winner in life's lottery, that we're 45
	The one who may yet be the next MacTrump,
	Or, at the least, will not become the chump
	To whom MacTrump severely shouts, "You're fired!"
	But there's the rub. It discounts history.
MacTRUMP	You are a loser. Evermore shall be. 50
O'BAMA	'Twas not the case in both oh-eight and twelve.
	I know because I won the both of them
	With a majority of pop'lar vote.

Enter GHOST OF BILLIAM O'CLINTON.

O'CLINTON	O, be you not too brutal with him, Banqy.
MacTRUMP	O'Clinton? You have a ghost too?
O'CLINTON	—Relax, 55
	Ex-presidents all have one whilst we live—
	It cometh from the Former Presidents
	Act pass'd in 1958.
MacTRUMP	—Indeed?
O'CLINTON	Indeed! It was a rider added by
	Ol' L. B. Jamy. He lik'd working nights. 60
MacTRUMP	Well, I have no idea who that man is,

	But if I hear you right, you do report
	That I shall one day have mine own ghost, too?
O'CLINTON	To be plain . . .
MacTRUMP	—What?
O'CLINTON	—We are not certain yet.
MacTRUMP	But wherefore not?
O'CLINTON	—What you must understand— 65

Enter GHOST OF RICHARD THE WORST.

RICHARD	The law applieth but to presidents
	Who never had themselves remov'd from office—
	Which was, I'll warrant, nearly my fate, too.
O'CLINTON	Believe me, Lord MacTrump—I feel your pain!
MacTRUMP	O, fame come to my room! You, sir, are Richard 70
	The Worst? You look e'en worse than that tattoo
	Of you that Blackstone hath upon his back.
RICHARD	Yes. I . . . shall never understand that man.

Enter GHOSTS OF GEORGE THE GREATER
and GEORGE THE LESSER.

GREATER	Alas, I know that fervent type too well.
	MacTrump, I know the people you work with, 75
	And they were ever hatchet men of woe.
LESSER	Thou hast it, Dad. 'Tis they who also made
	Me president: crooks, scoundrels, and turd blossoms
	Each one of them.
GREATER	—They did divide the country
	In ways that made your presence possible. 80
MacTRUMP	What of it? Would you have me give you thanks?

Depart, please, all of you—I fain would sleep.

Enter GHOST OF THEODORE ROSSEVELT.

T. ROSSEVELT   It shall take more than words to stop a bull moose!
                Have you no care for our environment?
                You wantonly destroy or do permit   85
                Destruction of all that is beautiful.
                You turn our streams and rivers into sewers,
                Pollute the air, destroy the forests, and
                Exterminate our fishes, birds, and mammals—
                To utter naught of vulgarizing charming   90
                Terrain with hideous advertisements!
MacTRUMP   If 'tis my great casinos you imply,
                They were the only decent thing in Jersey.
FALSTAFT   [*offstage:*] I disagree! I've suffer'd your buffet.
MacTRUMP   Who said that?

                Thudding footsteps approach.
                Enter GHOST OF WILLIAM FALSTAFT.

FALSTAFT   —I once dedicated time   95
                As both chief justice and, within these halls,
                As president protecting citizens
                From businessmen-conspirators like you!
                Forsooth, I busted twice the trusts as my
                Friend Teddy here. Were I chief justice now,   100
                I would, with glee, look forward to presiding
                O'er your impeachment.
T. ROSSEVELT   [*to Falstaft:*]   —Bully for you, William!
MacTRUMP   I shall be honest: I am most afraid

Of mine impeachment, yet not half as scar'd
As I am of Putain. The man is tough.   105
Methinks there's no one who could best his might.

Enter GHOST OF FRANKLIN ROSSEVELT.

F. ROSSEVELT	The only thing to fear is fear itself!
MACTRUMP	Wait, wait—were you not in a wheelchair bound?
F. ROSSEVELT	I did not need the use of my two legs
	To stand against our fascist foes abroad. 110
	I bested them whilst your own father, sir,
	Hoped that their master race would rule the world!
MACTRUMP	Pray, watch your mouth, you sniv'ling, whither'd
	wimp.
	My father march'd with Klansmen, not with nuts!
	It's Democrati who are socialists. 115

Enter GHOSTS OF HARRY S. TRUEMAN,
DWIGHT D. EISENPOWER, *and* RONALD REGAN.

TRUEMAN	The buck stops here!
REGAN	—You call yourself a good
	Republicon? I favor'd gun control,
	Applauded immigration, and commanded
	The Prussians to tear down their wall, MacTrump!
EISENPOWER	You owe each man and woman in our forces 120
	A grand apology for ev'ry insult
	You hurl'd toward our prisoners of war.
	Apologize to them, and then resign!
MACTRUMP	Ha, ha, you jest! I never shall resign.
	If trouble comes, I'll grant myself a pardon. 125

RICHARD   I tried to do that once. It workèd not.
MacTRUMP   Fie, out! You wretched souls, give me my rest!
                        [All exeunt except MacTrump, who
                                awakes from his nightmare.
              O, I have had a most rare vision here—
              A dream, past wit to say what dream it was.
              I'd be an ass, if I'd expound this dream.
              Methought I was—there's none who can tell what.   130
              The eye of man, I'll warrant, hath not heard,
              The ear of man hath never seen, man's hand
              May never taste, his tongue cannot conceive,
              Nor his heart to report, what my dream was.
              Am I the lowest 'mongst the presidents?   135
              Nay! Never! All these shadows have offended,
              For none compare unto the great MacTrump!
              I am the greatest president in hist'ry,
              E'en blowing Ronnie Regan far away.
              [*Calling:*] McTweet!

                    Enter McTweet.

McTWEET   —A midnight summons! 'Tis
                                        your wont.   140
MacTRUMP   Write something—anything—about how I
              Am far superior to those before.
              All those past presidents were hacks and wimps.
                        [McTweet begins writing quickly.
              'Tis only through MacTrump the office shines—
              Ne'er did the sun shine brighter than today!   145
McTWEET   [*aside:*] A-ha, then he admits to global warming?
MacTRUMP   No president e'er harder work'd than me,

To clean the mess that I inherited!
Say more besides—make up whate'er thou wilt.

McTWEET You'd have me autogenerate your words? 150

MacTRUMP Thou hast my trust, I gave thee my covfefe.

McTWEET 'Twill be done as you say, lord. One thing more . . .

MacTRUMP Yea?

McTWEET —Have you seen the news that's trending now?

MacTRUMP Is't good or bad? I prithee, make it good.

McTWEET The good or bad is what you make of it— 155
Your enemies, methinks, would call it good.

MacTRUMP Alas! Pray, tear the bandage off in haste!

McTWEET Your former lawyer LaCöhen doth work
With the MacMueller inquisition, giving
His full cooperation to their task. 160
Your children, too, are under some suspicion
For sharing information sensitive
E'en via mine own self, McTweet.

MacTRUMP —O, heavens!
Base LaCöhen, the flap-mouth'd fool-born lout!
McTweet, thou art a nuisance, get thee gone— 165
But do my bidding also, post my missives!

McTWEET Sir, there hath also been another shooting—

MacTRUMP O, who hath time for this? Send forth some words.

McTWEET It shall be done.

[Exit McTweet.

MacTRUMP —Curse this most wretched night,
Wherein I have been so unfairly us'd 170
By ghosts and nightmares, news and rank reports.
My sleep is troubl'd, as it has been e'er
Since Robert of MacMueller entered on
The scene, with inquisition most unfair.

As I said when I first learn'd of his probe,   175
The same is true today: 'tis terrible,
Belike the ending of my presidency.
I'm fubb'd off, well and truly, should he find
A trace of all the misdeeds I have done.
The task is mine, to shore up my support,   180
For public sentiment is ev'rything.
With public sentiment, there's naught can fail;
Without it, nothing can succeed. I must
Continue to pursue my wall, which sets
My base into a frenzy of delight.   185
Now, though, I need to rest my eyes awhile,
Or I will crack beneath this pressure harsh.
'Tis pitiful when even history
And all the sordid characters thereof
Pursue me past the warm embrace of sleep.   190
Alas, I'm still afeard of what I saw.
Perhaps my lady shall some comfort proffer.
               [He looks to the other side of the bed.
My lady? Art thou sleeping? Wilt thou wake?
I have had visions most severe this night.
               [He realizes Lady MacTrump is not there.
Of course, what was I thinking? She and I   195
Have not slept in one bed as couples do
For well-nigh seven months. She says I snore.
It also seemeth that our love doth shrink.
How fondly I recall her sweet embrace,
Which, like a mother's, quickly calms my soul.   200
How gladly would I welcome her in bed
To talk me through these daunting slings and arrows.
Yet wishing cannot bring the lady here—

And I'll not stoop to summon her to bed.
'Tis odd—I have not seen her since the morn,   205
When on the balcony we watch'd the sky.
She did depart, belike in some distress?
Whatever. I have neither time nor wish
To carry her afflictions and mine own.
Still, would I had her bosom here with me . . .   210
Enow! I must attempt to sleep once more—
Ye ghosts and phantoms, stay outside the door!

ACT
IV

SCENE 1.

In the Oval Tower.

Enter CHORUS.

CHORUS   Disturb'd and fitful nights besiege the realm,
              From commoners to senators to kings—
              For when MacTrump is seated at the helm,
              All worry over what the morrow brings.
              Great Fooliani tries to calm the tide,   5
              Yet only steers the ship to stranger seas.
              The people, all aboard this sick'ning ride,
              Are blown about by ev'ry little breeze.
              In anguish doth MacTrump turn to his staff—
              The ministers and keen advisors who   10
              Should cut his worries and concerns by half,
              And help him smoother waters to pursue.
              Upon a stormy ocean sails our ship—
              Will it change course, or 'neath the water slip?

Enter VICEROY MICHAEL POUND, LADY KELLEYANNE BOLEYN,
SIR MICHAEL POMPEII, *and* LADY SARAH PUCKABEE. *Enter* SIR
JOHN MACKEELEY *with them, calling them all to order. They
all hold copies of the* New Yorktown Times *newspaper.*

MacKEELEY   Good gentles, many thanks for coming quickly.   15
              Ye all, no doubt, have seen the letter vicious
              About bold President MacTrump within
              The pages of the false *New Yorktown Times,*

From some audacious and suspicious knave
Purporting to be part of the resistance   20
Inside of the MacTrump administration.
As one who works beside the president,
I made a vow with you, like-minded colleagues,
To thwart the baser parts of his agenda,
And his worst inclinations, yet this letter   25
Cannot be tolerated in the least!
As aide-de-camp, I'll root its author out.

POUND   This letter is, in faith, a threat'ning canker
Unto our lodestar President MacTrump.
'Tis not the inquisition looming large,   30
Or that the country's bitterly divided,
Or that our party may expect to lose
The Southern Chamber to an opposition
Hellbent upon his downfall. Nay, the problem—
Which even he still doth not fully grasp—   35
Is that full many of the senior members
Of his administration work with craft
To frustrate portions of his plans and schemes.
We all should know, for we are five of them.
Whoe'er hath writ the letter must, anon,   40
Show honor—yea, they must resign forthwith.

PUCKABEE   To be clear, Viceroy Pound, sir, ours is not
The popular resistance of the left.
We all desire th'administration to
Succeed and think its many policies   45
Already make America far safer
And far more prosperous than 'twas before.

POUND   Hear, hear!
KELLEYANNE   —Plusgood!

POMPEII   —I could not more agree.

PUCKABEE   Yet we believe our duty primary

Is to this country, and the president   50

Continueth to act in such a manner

That may be detrimental to the health

Of our republic noble. Ne'ertheless,

The most atrocious and deceitful coward

Who wrote this piece against the president   55

Is th'only one complicit in this act.

We five, in faith, do stand united and

Give all support to President MacTrump.

POMPEII   As any of us present understand,

The problem is his amorality.   60

We who do work with him know he's not moor'd

To a discernible first principle

That could inform his making of decisions.

Of course, my friends, the letter is not mine.

'Tis no surprise the vile *New Yorktown Times*,   65

Which hath attack'd MacTrump relentlessly,

Would print a piece like this one—a disgruntl'd,

Deceptive actor's word—'tis passing sad.

If one would not obey the chief's intent,

There is an option singular: to leave.   70

The media's attempts to undermine

Our bold administration in this way

Are no less than incredibly disturbing.

KELLEYANNE   'Tis certain our successes come despite

The president's rare style of leadership,   75

Which is impetuous and petty, yea—

Both adversarial and ineffective.

Yet I'm not sure the letter even matters—

Thoughtcrimes do flow through the *New Yorktown*
Times
Each day, withal a diff'rent byline or, 80
In this case, nonbyline. It is unclear
'Twas even written by the White Hold staff.

MacKEELEY Despite the early whispers in the cab'net
That they might launch a mission to invoke
The twenty-fifth commandment—and begin 85
A process to remove the president—
None wish'd to start a governmental crisis.
Thus, we will do whate'er we can to steer
Th'administration in the right direction
Until—one way or other—it is over. 90
If I do hear aright, we are agreed—
Though meetings with the president may veer
Off topic quickly and, then, off the rails,
And he doth sputter rants repetitive,
And his impulsiveness resulteth in 95
Half-bak'd and ill-inform'd and sometimes reckless
Decisions that must, later, be walk'd back,
And though there literally is no telling
If he may change his ever-shifting mind
One minute to the next—we unsung heroes 100
Stand proudly and salute our mighty chief,
Maintain our right and proper chain of c'mmand,
And with one voice reject this hateful letter.

ALL Forsooth!

Enter MacTRUMP, *with* FOOLIANI *at his heel.*
Others quickly try to hide their newspapers.

MacKEELEY	—Good morning, Master President.
MacTRUMP	Pray, wipe the false smile off thine brown-nos'd

face. 105

MacKEELEY	Beg pardon, sir—
MacTRUMP	[*mocking:*] —"Beg pardon, sir, beg pardon."

Well mayst thou beg a pardon of me soon.

> [*He pulls out a copy of the* New Yorktown
>   Times, *waving it in MacKeeley's face.*

It is a sorry, scrawny aide-de-camp
Who cannot keep a letter such as this
From being spread around the land entire.   110
Methought when I did choose a general,
I pick'd a man of strength and leadership,
Yet now 'tis absolutely clear than e'en
My treasurer—who is more dolt than man—
Would do a better job than thou hast done.   115
What hast thou done to stop MacMueller, hind?
The inquisition moveth forward like
A rabid bull toward the reddest cape!

MacKEELEY	I have fulfill'd the duties of mine office

Unto the best of my abilities.   120

MacTRUMP	Then thine abilities are sorely lacking.
PUCKABEE	We shall at once release a statement, sir,

Decrying this foul letter and its author—

MacTRUMP	What good are these, thy statements and thy cries?

Thou standest at the podium an 'twere   125
A deer who stoppeth 'fore the headlamps' glow.
The press do frighten thee—thou art no bulwark
Against the rising tide of public scorn.

PUCKABEE	Perhaps we'll get you on the Pox Network—

A guest appearance would repair this breach.   130

MacTRUMP	How canst thou place reliance on faux news?
	Wouldst thou make this foul situation worse?
	The media is naught but thieves and anglers.
POMPEII	Sir, if you would—
MacTRUMP	—Do not begin to speak,
	Thou who wouldst take the credit for my good 135
	Relations with the North Korasian leader.
POMPEII	[*aside:*] Had I not done some swift maneuvering,
	The situation dire with King John Ill
	Might once have brought the country to a war!
	MacTrump, however, cannot hear that truth. 140
KELLEYANNE	I bid you, Master President, is there
	Aught we can do for you? Your temper doth
	Appear to be most plusbad presently.
MacTRUMP	Thou wench! Canst thou not stop thy husband's
	tongue?
	He is the biggest critic that I have. 145
	Where thou shouldst help me, thou dost naught but
	hurt,
	Thou strumpet, sleeping with the enemy!
KELLEYANNE	O, Master President!
MacTRUMP	—'Tis but the truth.
POUND	Pray, sir, be calm. We do but try to help.
MacTRUMP	Et tu, Pound? Thou art worst of all the rest. 150
	First thou didst near abandon me when thou
	Didst learn of my distinctive ways with women
	Whilst the election was at its high point.
	Now thou sitt'st silently in meetings if
	The outcome could be thou succeeding me. 155
	[*To all:*] You all are miserable comforters!
	This clown, great Fooliani, could direct

The country with far more success than you.

In sooth, the notion holds a strong allure,

For Fooliani never did me wrong.   160

'Til further notice, you are all dismiss'd—

I'll let him rule the White Hold in your place!

Pray, get you gone!

MACKEELEY   [*aside to Pompeii:*] —The man is mad, 'tis plain!

POMPEII   [*aside to MacKeeley:*] The third time he hath fir'd us

all this month.

[*Exeunt all but MacTrump and Fooliani.*

FOOLIANI   Last time I saw you clear a room so fast,   165

'Twas after you had eaten beef sorbet.

MACTRUMP   Come Fooliani, cheer mine angry heart.

Thou ever wert amusing, by my troth.

Dost thou have some smart riddle for to share?

FOOLIANI   In sooth, my whole career hath been a riddle.   170

Here's one that shall enlighten your dark mood:

Do you know, nuncle, when a thing's no thing?

MACTRUMP   If 'tis a thing, then it must be a thing,

Yet if 'tis no thing, it must no thing be.

I cannot solve thy riddle, 'tis too hard.   175

How can a thing be no thing, Fooliani?

FOOLIANI   When 'tis collusion.

[*Fooliani shakes his marotte.*

Bells jingle.

MACTRUMP   —Speak thou not that word!

I told thee ne'er to say the C-word, knave!

FOOLIANI   Methinks you have misunderstood my wit.

Collusion, sir, is no thing.

MACTRUMP   —Isn't it?   180

FOOLIANI   To do a thing illegal is a crime,

And it is said collusion is a crime—
It follows, then, collusion is illegal.
Yet have you ever read a definition
Of that most sly and sneaky word, collusion?   185
The word may speak of some agreements secret,
Yet do not even spouses share such things?
The meaning doth include cooperation,
Yet is not that a good and worthy thing?
The definition may speak of deceit,   190
Yet who hath never spake a little lie?
Illegal, though? Show me the dictionary!
If I am wrong, pray throw the book at me.
Collusion's not illegal, liege. Not if
Old Merriam and Webster have their way.   195
And if 'tis not illegal, 'tis no crime,
But if 'tis said collusion is a crime,
Yet 'tis no crime, it cancels out itself—
For it cannot be both a crime and no crime!
Thus, like a number that is added to   200
An equal number, but its negative,
The end result is zero. Do you see?
Collusion is the thing that is no thing.

MACTRUMP   Steady, thou hast a dizzying intellect,
Yet all the same I find thee brilliant. Ha!   205
Collusion is the thing that is no thing!

FOOLIANI   [*singing:*] Collusion is the thing that is no thing!
                  Yea, let our voices ever with it ring,

BOTH   [*singing:*] Above the mountaintops we gladly sing,
                  Unto this truth we two shall ever cling,   210
                  A better future it doth with it bring,
                  Shout it unto the peasant and the king,

                    Tell it to both the lib'rals and right wing—
                      Collusion is the thing that is no thing!

MacTRUMP   Thou art a balm unto my weary soul,   215
                    My thanks, Great Fooliani! Yea, for thou
                    Hast made me all my hindrances forget.
                    I'll make thee my attorney gen'ral yet!

                                      [Exeunt, laughing.

SCENE 2.

In the White Hold.

Enter DAME DESDIVANKA.

DESDIVANKA   The best of plans cannot o'ercome mistakes,
                    And in the latest instance, they were made.
                    My machinations sly shall ne'er succeed
                    When errors do surround me constantly.
                    MacMueller, stripping me of liberty,   5
                    Did have the gall to spy upon me whilst
                    I spake about the meeting with the Prussians
                    That, once, my brothers took in Tow'r MacTrump.
                    He presseth even further on we siblings,
                    Investigating now the Moskvá Tow'r   10
                    We hop'd to build before our father was
                    The leader of the new world. Out upon't!
                    MacMueller is a thorn in each our sides
                    That I would gladly pull out with my teeth.

Alack, the man is well protected, ring'd   15
With pow'rful friends, attentive to the public,
And expert at his inquisition game.
I may not do to him as I might wish,
But, peradventure, I can close the breach
Within our citadel ere 'tis too late.   20
And, speaking of mistakes, here come my brothers—
They'll have a piece of Desdivanka's mind.

Enter DONNISON *and* ERICSON.

DONNISON	The word was *laurel*—
ERICSON	—Nay, 'twas truly *yanny*!
DESDIVANKA	My brothers, come and talk with me awhile.
ERICSON	Are we in trouble?
DONNISON	—Ericson, poor fool. 25

Sweet Desdivanka is our loving sister—
She's not our mother come to scold us. Ha!
"Are we in trouble?" What a childish thought.
Is not that funny, sister?

DESDIVANKA	—I shall take

As many laughs therefrom as thou mayst take   30
Upon a knife's point, choke a daw withal.

DONNISON	I chok'd a what?
DESDIVANKA	—O, you two jackanapes!

You are too careless by a hectare's breadth.
The messages you're sending through McTweet
Are being intercepted by our foes!   35
How do you think MacMueller came to know
About the meeting with the Prussians when
We made our stand against Hillaria?

You man-boys need to learn to use your heads—
It is the lump three feet above your arses!   40
You shall bring Father infamous disgrace,
Dishonor on the family entire,
If you shall never think ere you do act!

DONNISON   O, sister, have we wrong'd our father so?

ERICSON   Apologies aplenty, Desdivanka.   45

DESDIVANKA   Apologies—fie! Your apologies
Are empty words come forth from empty heads.
'Tis not words of repentance I desire—
You must begin to take bold action to
Redress the wrongs you have, of late, committed,   50
Thus to reside within our father's grace.

DONNISON   What shall we do? Pray tell!

DESDIVANKA   —For one, cease all
Communication through the tool McTweet,
Who is a vulture and stool pigeon both,
An albatross tied tightly round your necks!   55

ERICSON   E'en following the latest hashtag trends?

DESDIVANKA   Thou'lt soon see #fratricide begin to trend,
If thou canst not do what I say.

                            [Ericson gulps.

ERICSON   —I shall.

DESDIVANKA   Be sure you do.

DONNISON   —I know how we may help.
Our father is near purple in the face   60
Each time he talketh of his border wall.
Mayhap young Ericson and I can help—
We'll travel south and build the wall ourselves!

DESDIVANKA   [*aside:*] An imbecile's idea. Yet if it shall
Get these astounding fools out of the way,   65

I'll swear it is inspir'd by heav'n above.

[*To Donnison:*] A notion excellent in the extreme.

How soon, wise brother, can you two depart?

ERICSON   The sooner gone, the sooner done.

DONNISON   —Forsooth!

Come, brother, let us southward turn our faces.   70

ERICSON   Where we shall build our father's wall with pride.

BOTH   A-thump, a-thump, here come MacTrumps!

DESDIVANKA   —Go, then,

And with ye both a sister's fondest hopes.

                [Exeunt Donnison and Ericson.

Poor folly-fallen baggages, these boys—

A wonder 'tis we from the same womb sprung.   75

I would near pity them, were they not such

Inestimable fools. Let them unto

Our southern border go, whilst I shore up

The Southern Chamber for the next election.

Republicons therein are all dimwitted,   80

Mere parvenus who rode to pow'r atop

The backs of paper tigers, snollygosters,

Teabaggers, chicken hawks, and Prussian trolls.

They nothing know of passing laws or how

One may repeal rank, overreaching acts.   85

Their only expertise is taking cash

And shaming Democrati presidents.

O'Bama, though, is gone and shan't return.

Sans him, these full-gorg'd dolts are useless as

A bastard scabbard made without a slit.   90

They do accomplish nothing, proffer less,

And their most gallant speaker's nothing but

A toothless babe who was untimely wean'd.

To ev'ry jot of power I shall cling,
And shall, anon, take over ev'rything.   95
                                        [*Exit.*

SCENE 3.

In the Oval Tower.

Enter CZAR VLAD PUTAIN *above, on balcony.*

PUTAIN   MacTrump, my droog, perhaps was a mistake.
                He is sufficiently unscrupulous,
                As any tool of mine abroad must be,
                Yet he is also unreliable,
                Far weaker than I did anticipate.   5
                The inclination of his heart is evil,
                And I regret I made him what he is.
                The time hath come to rectify the matter.
                [*Calling:*] McTweet, come forth!
McTWEET   —Da, comrade?
PUTAIN   —Send
                                                the bots.
                MacTrump too long hath focus'd inward only.   10
                Make him to know there is an outer flank—
                An international community—
                That happily will goad him while he rests.
                Be certain King XI Ping and King John Ill
                Do stand prepar'd for all that lies ahead.   15

Turn even allies—like Justin Truebeau,
Andrés Matador, He-Manuel Macroon—
Into a bother for the president.

McTWEET   One universal firestorm, coming up.

[Exit McTweet.

PUTAIN   The wheels are set in motion: I shall watch   20
As Europe falls apart through doubt and fear.
Sweet dreams, MacTrump. The world doth come for
thee.

[Exit Putain from balcony.

Enter MᴀᴄTʀᴜᴍᴘ, Sɪʀ Jᴏʜɴ MᴀᴄKᴇᴇʟᴇʏ,
and Sɪʀ Mɪᴄʜᴀᴇʟ Pᴏᴍᴘᴇɪɪ.

MᴀᴄTRUMP   Pray, tell me once again what is the haps?
POMPEII   Vast pressure from the nations of the world
Hath lately risen up. Our allies global   25
Are worried o'er the comments you releas'd
Before the summit of Globe7 leaders.
Thou didst declare, "Prime Minister Truebeau
Is ever so indignant over us,
Yet speaks not of how Qanada doth charge   30
Our dairy farmers, hurting agriculture."
He is a friend of Macroon, he of France,
Who taketh to McTweet his sage advice,
That "isolationism is a threat
Unto the people of America."   35
He then invokes your noble name itself,
Declaring, "President MacTrump knows that."
The largest problem, though, is King XI Ping—
Who doth, as you know, lead the Middle Kingdom—

               Although you did grant him a visit, sir,   40
               He standeth resolutely 'gainst our hopes
               That we may seek a fairer route to trade.
               He stops at nothing to protect his int'rests,
               Which, ev'ry year, hurt our economy.

MacTRUMP   Cease blathering—thou lost me at "vast pressure."   45
               I've told thee this before: make it more simple.

MacKEELEY   World: angry. King XI Ping: bad. Problem: big.
                  [MacKeeley holds up a picture of Eurasia,
                  on which the Middle Kingdom is marked by
                  red arrows and has an X drawn through it.

MacTRUMP   At last, a briefing I can understand!
               We levy tariffs on the Middle Kingdom,
               On Qanada and Mexitlán as well,   50
               And ev'ry nation of Europa, too!

POMPEII   This shall enrage our allies dreadfully.
               Methinks this plan will have vast repercussions.

MacTRUMP   Didst thou e'er build a business from the ground?

POMPEII   Nay, sir, yet—

MacTRUMP   —Art thou skill'd in ways of commerce? 55

POMPEII   The international—

MacTRUMP   —Methought not—when
               A country like the great United Fiefdoms
               Is losing many billions on our trade
               With virtually ev'ry country we
               Do business with, I say: trade wars are good.   60
               Moreover, they are effortless to win.
               Example: when we're down one hundred billion
               With certain countries and they would be coy,
               We trade no more—we win big. Easy 'tis!

[Pompeii is aghast and falls silent,
with his mouth open.

MacKEELEY　　The tariffs shall be set in motion, sir.　　　　65

MacTRUMP　　What of Pompeii? It seems he may erupt.

MacKEELEY　　He shall be fine.

[MacKeeley takes Pompeii by
the arm to help him leave.

MacTRUMP　　　　　　　　—MacKeeley, ere thou goest.

MacKEELEY　　Yea, Lord MacTrump?

MacTRUMP　　　　　　　　　　—Bid Robert Wormwood come.

MacKEELEY　　It shall be done.

[Exeunt MacKeeley guiding
the shocked Pompeii.

MacTRUMP　　　　　　　　—My head is sore with care.

This situation international　　　　　　　　70
Is more than I can bear—or understand.
Combin'd with the MacMueller inquisition
And Democrati foes who rear their heads,
I'll gladly speak with Robert, whom I've known
For decades, ere I was the president.　　　　75
Besides, this Wormwood's book may boost my woes
If he doth paint a picture bleak of me.
The people, for whatever reason, seem
To put excessive stock in his faux news.
Mayhap I shall convince him to relent　　　　80
Of any bad—and false—report he'd make.

Enter ROBERT WORMWOOD.

WORMWOOD　　Good even, Master President. You rang?

MacTRUMP　　Holla, Robert, my thanks that thou didst come.

WORMWOOD   Of course, sir. I'll record our conversation,
                If 'tis acceptable.

MacTRUMP   —Indeed, indeed.   85

                [Wormwood pulls out a quill to begin writing.

WORMWOOD   How may I help thee, President MacTrump?

MacTRUMP   I sit here, pond'ring over yesteryear.
                Remember when we spoke, an age ago,
                Whilst in the Tow'r MacTrump?

WORMWOOD   —I do, indeed.

MacTRUMP   By now, 'tis twenty years ago, at least.   90
                Thou wert, back then, considering a book
                That thou wouldst write about my simple life—
                Successful businessman and slick tycoon.
                Who would have thought these moons and orbits since
                That thou wouldst pen a very diff'rent book?   95
                Thy new book was not in the cards back then.

WORMWOOD   'Tis pity my book could not diff'rent be.
                Know that I spake with many people, sir,
                Thus to present a whole full and fair account.

MacTRUMP   'Tis well.

WORMWOOD   —You know, sir, we are living in   100
                A pivot point in history, methinks.

MacTRUMP   Alas that thou couldst not have talk'd with me.
                Thou knowest I am open e'er for thee.
                A most fair man thou art, for a news man.
                We shall see what transpires for thou and me.   105
                The country, as thou know'st, is faring well,
                The strong economy hath ris'n beyond
                All other eras in our nation's past.
                The unemployment numbers sink so low,
                That it shall soon be six feet under, ha!   110

	Large companies return to UF soil,	
	Which was unthinkable two years ago.	
WORMWOOD	I understand your point of view. Know this:	
	I've written books on eight past presidents,	
	From Richard th'Worst to Lord Banquo O'Bama,	115
	And have learn'd something of reporting, see—	
	As if your presidency were a house,	
	One must stand outside it to see the whole.	
	'Tis not by talking solely unto you,	
	Which opportunity I was denied,	120
	That I shall learn the most about you, sir.	
	I must see from the outside, and discuss	
	These topics far from people's offices—	
	'Tis there I gain both documents and insight.	
	The book I writ of you doth frankly look	125
	At three main themes: the globe entire today,	
	Your full administration, and yourself.	
MACTRUMP	Thou sayest it sans saying it at all:	
	I take it 'tis a negative report.	
	Yet I am half accustom'd to such things—	130
	The half of me that's harden'd to the world.	
	Some that is writ of me is bad, some good—	
	This one shall be a bad one, verily.	
WORMWOOD	'Twas chance that did deny the chance to speak—	
MACTRUMP	Communication here is far too chancy.	135
WORMWOOD	The book is transcrib'd carefully by scribes—	
	And bas'd upon real incidents.	
MACTRUMP	—O, Robert,	
	Dost thou know I am doing a great job?	
WORMWOOD	The book is factual and accurate.	
MACTRUMP	'Tis accurate that I am doing great—	140

No one has ever done as well as I.

WORMWOOD   Hear, Master President: I do believe
In our United Fiefdoms and, as such,
I wish you ev'ry fortune in all things.

MACTRUMP   My thanks. Farewell.

[*Exit Wormwood.*]

Enter McTWEET.

McTWEET   —My lord, a word.

MACTRUMP   —Alas,   145
I did not bid thee come. An thou art here,
It means some dreadful news befalls myself.
Pray, tell me quickly.

McTWEET   —Trending even now:
The new book *Present Fears* by Robert Wormwood.
His tale of your administration doth   150
Both shock and madden people ev'rywhere.

MACTRUMP   Fie, fie upon it! Out, give me some air!

[*Exit McTweet.*]

Words! Sland'rous, cutting, overthrowing words!
How shall a man survive a surfeit of
Verbs, nouns, and prepositions thrown like knives,   155
Assailing him from ev'ry side? O, Wormwood!
Thy good opinion I so much desire—
Thou hast thy horrid words sicc'd on MacTrump.
That ever I should see this wretched day.
Would I could make return unto the past,   160
When mine affairs were not affairs of state,
When I could spend a night with Tempest Daniels
And no one car'd or thought to care a whit.

O for a simpler time, with fewer words.
This book shall ruin sleep, though I do need it—   165
To think that I shall never even read it!

> *[Exit.*

SCENE 4.

Columbia Island. Across the river from Washingtown.

Enter DONNISON *and* ERICSON *agallop.*

ERICSON Are we there yet? O, have we reach'd the south?
DONNISON Methinks we must have, brother. We have trotted
Through Washingtown at least an hour or more.
ERICSON Where is the river?
DONNISON —We just cross'd its banks.
See thou the bridge that now is far behind us?   5

> *[Ericson turns around.*

ERICSON A-ha! So that is what 'twas. Brother, thanks!
Let us dismount t'embrace the southern land
That Father captur'd so triumphantly.
DONNISON Avast!

> *[The brothers stop galloping. Donnison*
> *steps forward and throws his arms out.*

ERICSON —Behold the land, mine elder kin!
The fertile southern fiefdom of . . . [*He reads a road*
sign.] Vagina?   10
DONNISON 'Tis Virginía, Ericson.

ERICSON   —Of course!

DONNISON   The Virginía colony: the neighbor
                  Of presidents, the Old Derision, too.
                  We shall begin to build our father's wall,
                  Here on the southern side of th'Rio Grundy.   15

ERICSON   A plan fantastic, older sibling wise!
                  What shall we build it with?

DONNISON   —I do not know.
                  What of those stones?

ERICSON   —Where?

DONNISON   —Yonder, down the
                                                    road.
                                  [Donnison points off.

ERICSON   Methinks not, brother, for that cemetery
                  Is hallow'd such that not e'en our bold father   20
                  Will set a foot therein.

DONNISON   —Yea, point well ta'en.
                  We shall persist with what we haply scrounge,
                  And build one of those stonewalls Father's lawyers
                  Are so well-known for.

ERICSON   —Wonderful idea!
                  Shall we dig through the dirt to find some stones? 25

DONNISON   E'en better: what if thou dost dig for stones
                  Whilst I observe?

ERICSON   —My toil in soil beginneth!
                          [Ericson starts digging but is interrupted
                                  by the sounds of protestors chanting.

PROTESTORS   [offstage:] No wall!

DONNISON   —Dost hear that sound?

ERICSON   —What?

DONNISON   —Take thou heed!

PROTESTORS [*offstage:*] No wall! No wall!

ERICSON —The voices cry, "No
wall."

DONNISON What luck! There must not be a wall at that 30
Location. Brother, come! Vacate your hole
That we may answer th'orisons of those
Demanding Father's mighty wall be built
Where there is none.

ERICSON —Let us away to help!
[*Exeunt Donnison and Ericson.*

Enter PROTESTORS *carrying signs, with*
MARIANNE *and* JUSTINE *among them.*

PROTESTORS No wall! No wall!

JUSTINE —The people speak as one. 35
It seems to me they want their country back.

MARIANNE We'll take it, too! MacTrump has unified
His foes against him. Now we stand united!

JUSTINE It is a welcome sign of things to come,
Yet we must also stand for one another. 40
A despot happily forgives his subjects
If they do love him not, provided they
Shall, in the bargain, like each other less.

MARIANNE I've not forgotten all thou taught'st me, sister.
The very liberties that we enjoy 45
Empower'd villains like MacTrump to seize
Our stage. No more! The weak Republicons
Will dearly pay for pledging him allegiance.
A blue wave builds! [*To protestors:*] Remember ye
November!

                   [All cheer.

JUSTINE   Wilt thou be speaking soon?

MARIANNE   —I'm next in line. 50

JUSTINE   Hast thou thy speech preparèd?

MARIANNE   —In a way—
I plan to march atop those stairs and speak
Whatever hell or heaven put inside me!

JUSTINE   It is thy right.

MARIANNE   —By all the gods, yea, 'tis!
To sin by silence when we should protest 55
Makes cowards out of men.

JUSTINE   —And women too.
Of course, such is their right—no matter how
Unhealthy or unwise their silence—when
Confronting despotism unrestrain'd.

MARIANNE   O sister dear, I hope thou shalt not chide 60
Thyself for thy decision not to speak?

JUSTINE   Nay, sister, ne'er. I merely do prefer
To listen. 'Tis, indeed, my liberty.

            [A protestor invites Marianne
               to the dais to speak.

MARIANNE   'Tis now my time to speak. Art thou most sure
That thou wouldst not be thereupon with me? 65

JUSTINE   Thou mak'st me laugh. I ever am with thee!
Please leave me here to cheer you on. Go, speak!

MARIANNE   If we are separated, call my name.

JUSTINE   Thou worriest too much o'er me. Be gone!

       [Justine playfully shoves Marianne toward
         the balcony. Marianne ascends.

Enter DONNISON *and* ERICSON.

ERICSON	Ah, here! The people who desire our wall. 70
DONNISON	Indeed! Start thou the work whilst I survey—
	[Donnison turns his head and sees
	Marianne addressing the crowd.
	Good brother, look!
ERICSON	—What is it?
DONNISON	—It is she,
	The woman of my dreams, my secret love!
ERICSON	Zounds. Thou art right, my brother! And behold,
	There standeth my belovèd 'mongst the mob, 75
	As stalwart as a wall of stone herself!
DONNISON	Snapsooth! This is the moment, patient hunter.
	Our search is over! No more messages
	Or pesky tweets. Our trophies we have found,
	Now let us win them! Thither to thy love 80
	And woo her whilst I watch and wait for mine
	To finish speaking.
ERICSON	—O, 'tis happening.
	Away I go! Bless us!
DONNISON	—Good fortune, brother!
	[Ericson moves through the crowd toward
	Justine, whose attention remains fixed
	on Marianne. Once he is close, Ericson
	clears his throat and stands next to her
	while Donnison watches from behind.
ERICSON	*[to Justine:]* Our fates are blessèd, lass.
	[Justine does not respond.
	Tell me, doth Deb—
MARIANNE	No wall!
JUSTINE	—No wall!
ERICSON	—Indeed! There is no wall. 85

DONNISON   [*from behind:*] Keep at it, Ericson! Thou'rt faring
                       well!

ERICSON   [*to Justine, louder:*] Pray tell, dost thou do DC often,
                       Debbie?

JUSTINE   I beg thy pardon, sirrah, but wouldst thou
            Reduce the volume of thy voice? 'Tis loud.

ERICSON   Forgive me. Have I met thee once before?   90

JUSTINE   Good sir, I cannot say I've seen thee ere
            Because I know for certain I have not.

ERICSON   O . . . [*To Donnison:*] She call'd me "good sir"!

DONNISON   —Press
                      on, Adonis!

ERICSON   [*to Justine:*] My lady, 'tis a pleasure meeting thee.
            My name is Ericson. And you are call'd . . . ?   95
                [*Justine turns her head slightly.*

JUSTINE   Justine. I've heard thy voice before.

ERICSON   —Yea? Where?

JUSTINE   I am not sure. Liv'st thou in Washingtown?

ERICSON   Nay, nay. My family is from New Yorktown.

JUSTINE   Thou mad'st the journey hither for this protest?

ERICSON   In sooth! My brother and I just came south!   100

JUSTINE   'Tis most commendable.

ERICSON   —My thanks.

DONNISON   —Ha—gold!

ERICSON   Where art thou from?

JUSTINE   —'Tis tricky to pronounce.
            A group of islands call'd Ko Phi Phi.

ERICSON   [*aghast:*] Covfefe?!

JUSTINE   —Nay, thou heard'st wrong: 'tis Ko
                      Phi Phi.
            In Siam. 'Tis an archipelago.   105

ERICSON	A Michelangelo where thou didst live?
JUSTINE	[*laughing:*] I told thee difficult 'tis to pronounce!
ERICSON	That was most fair of thee! Thou art most just.
JUSTINE	Nay. Fairness isn't justice.
ERICSON	—Wait. In sooth?

I did not know the two were not the same.   110

JUSTINE	Few people do.

        [Marianne sees Justine and Ericson talking,
            ends her speech, and descends toward them.

MARIANNE	[*aside:*] —What is this?
JUSTINE	[*shouting to Marianne:*] —Brava, sister!
ERICSON	[*to Justine:*] Are you two siblings?
JUSTINE	—Nay, mere

                              roommates we.

Although she is like family to me.

ERICSON	Before I meet her, prithee know, Justine,

That meeting thee hath giv'n me total joy.   115

Again, I'm Ericson.

JUSTINE	—Of House MacTrump?

My memory hath caught up to thy voice.

ERICSON	Indeed—'tis me!
JUSTINE	[*aside:*] —This shall be interesting.

        [Marianne storms toward Ericson.

MARIANNE	What art thou doing here? Avaunt, thou snake!

        [Marianne pulls Justine away.

JUSTINE	There is no need to quarrel, sister, please. 120
ERICSON	[*to Donnison:*] Dear brother, is this good?
DONNISON	—Nay, sans

                             a doubt.

        [He leaps forward from his hiding place.

My dears, 'tis well to see you both again!

MARIANNE	Again? Are you two stalking us? Be gone!
JUSTINE	O sister, please! I was but speaking with
	One of them now.
MARIANNE	—Thou art confus'd or mad— 125
	Thou canst not see the things I have in view.
DONNISON	My lady, if I may—
MARIANNE	—Do not presume
	To call me aught of thine, thou foolborn twit!
JUSTINE	Nay, Marianne! I may be blind to th'world,
	Yet am not deaf to it. I know who these 130
	Men are. They are the issue of MacTrump:
	The brothers Ericson and Donnison.
ERICSON	Indeed! 'Tis who we are.
DONNISON	[to Marianne:] —And I love thee!
	[The ladies turn to the brothers, shocked.
MARIANNE	Thou . . . lovest me?
JUSTINE	—Pray, sister, hold thy rage.
	[Marianne steps toward Donnison.
MARIANNE	How canst thou say thou lovest me, thou pig? 135
	Thou art a blight upon this wondrous nation!
	Thou knowest naught of liberty or justice,
	Nor art thou capable of feeling love.
	Thy father is the foulest criminal
	Our land has seen, and thou his minion foul! 140
DONNISON	Thy words are false! Most people love our father.
PROTESTOR 1	[pointing to the brothers:] Behold!
	[All the protestors look at the brothers.
DONNISON	—See?
	We are recogniz'd. [To protestors:] Holla!
PROTESTORS	Booo!
ERICSON	—Donnison, methinks we must depart.

MARIANNE   Yea! Get ye hence at once, vile villains!
                      [All protestors begin shouting at the brothers.

JUSTINE   [*to all:*]   —Halt!
                                              [All are quiet.

                We all were not created equal or   145
                Completely free by birth upon this globe.
                I did not choose my blindness any more
                Than these two brothers chose their father's line.
                I have no doubt they love their family
                With all their hearts, which is their sacred right.   150
                My sister and myself do love ours, too,
                Which is why we reject their father's wall,
                His policies, his conduct, and the way
                He doth mistreat his countrymen and -women.
                This is their father's fault, not all their own.   155

MARIANNE   Justine, thou dost forget whom thou defend'st.
                [*Aside:*] McTweet!

                      Enter McTweet.

McTWEET   —Thou rang'st, my mistress?

MARIANNE   —Do a search
                For missives with the most revolting words
                These brothers shar'd: each hateful jab they threw,
                Each immigrant they slander'd woefully,   160
                Each cat endanger'd that they slew and skinn'd.

McTWEET   I shall!
                      *[McTweet holds up a picture of the
                      brothers alongside animals they hunted.*

PROTESTORS   —Booo!

DONNISON   —Soft you now, the cat was deadly!

JUSTINE   Dear bird, please read the elder brother's words
               When he compar'd sweets to refugees.

McTWEET   At thy request.

                              [McTweet pulls out a scrap of paper
                                    and begins reading from it.
                              —"This image sayeth all.   165
               Cease with politic'lly correct agendas
               That do not put th'United Fiefdoms first."
               The picture shows a bowl of rainbow sweets,
               And reads: "If I'd a bowl of skittl'd candies
               And told thee three would kill thee on the spot,   170
               Wouldst take a handful? 'Tis Assyria's
               Great problem with their wicked refugees.
               O, make America most great again!"
                              [McTweet puts his paper down.
               Shall I display the refugees they fear'd?

JUSTINE   'Twill not be necessary. Thou mayst go.   175
                              [McTweet bows and exits.
               [*To the brothers:*] Hear ye: opinions and beliefs are
                                                            form'd,
               The heart enlarg'd, the human mind develop'd,
               By our reciprocal effect upon
               Each other. Your opinions were, I'll warrant,
               Inspir'd and shap'd by your love for your father.   180
               Yet there's a danger in those who would shut
               Themselves in their own heart's dark solitude—
               You close yourself unto the world around
               So much that you contribute to its ruin.
               Your love is poisoning the minds of those   185
               Who turn to you for wisdom and for guidance.
               Such is the love you forc'd upon our world,

Which is a love that I, and my dear sister,
And all those present have no wish to share.

PROTESTORS   Boo-urns! No wall! No wall!

ERICSON   —Nay!

DONNISON   —We have fail'd. 190

O, sorrow! Let us flee.

ERICSON   —Anon.

MARIANNE   —Not yet!

Before you fly unto your iv'ry tow'r,
May I suggest a way you may employ
The precious liberty you do enjoy?
Use your positions in your family—   195
Which are undemocratic, yea, but potent—
To make your reparations most sincere
To ev'ryone whom you did e'er insult;
Atone for failures and for wicked deeds,
Make plain—unto your father's followers,   200
Unto your fellow citizens, e'en to
MacMueller—all the pain you propagated.

DONNISON   If I do this, then wilt thou love me?

MARIANNE   —Nay!

[Donnison sobs.

JUSTINE   Love is not won by crossing off a list.

However, it shall demonstrate to all   205
That ye shall both defend our liberty
And do possess the needed wisdom, courage,
And temper'ment to heed the call of justice.

ERICSON   Thy words sound passing hard! My father is

A wondrous man, exemplar in the height.   210

JUSTINE   'Tis ye, then, who are blind.

DONNISON   —Yet we would have ye—

	No finer heads could hang upon our walls!
MARIANNE	We are no trophies to be won, you brutes!
JUSTINE	Come, Marianne, let us vote with our feet.

[Exeunt Justine and Marianne, with protestors.

ERICSON	O, brother, we have fail'd! Let us to Father 215
	And tell him of what we have seen today.
DONNISON	He shall be proud we built his wall for him.
ERICSON	I built his wall.
DONNISON	—Whatever, it is thirsty work,
	When we get home, let's call up Brovanaugh
	To come and drink a pack of beers with us. 220
	Methinks we still shall find another way
	To win the bleeding hearts of these two ladies!
ERICSON	Thou thinkest so? They seem'd most resolute.
DONNISON	They are but ladies—therefore changeable.
ERICSON	Hurrah!
DONNISON	—Unto the White Hold, let us ride— 225
	Full gallop, with our newfound hope beside!

[Exeunt.

SCENE 5.

The White Hold. Night.

Enter LADY KELLEYANNE BOLEYN, LADY SARAH
PUCKABEE, *and* DOCTOR PINO ENOS.

| ENOS | Why must you ladies summon me so late? |

My license, for to practice medicine,
Turns to a pumpkin at the stroke of midnight.
Thereafter, I am not allow'd within
Three hundred paces of a human body.   5

KELLEYANNE   All's plusgood, Doctor. Doubleplusgood, yea!
We merely doublethink the evening staff
May benefit from thy fullwise opinion
Upon the double-doubleplusgood state
Of our Lady MacTrump's goodthinkingness.   10

ENOS   Ma'am, I have no idea what thou hast said.

PUCKABEE   She sayeth that we need thy help, good doctor,
And if thou dost not mind me speaking bluntly,
Methinks thou art far better company
Amid the daylight hours, and far less rude.   15

ENOS   'Tis certain, for the daytime's when I work;
When it is night, I spend my time asleep.
Why have ye brought me hither, ladies? Why?

> *[Puckabee and Kelleyanne*
> *trade anxious glances.*

PUCKABEE   Aught is awry with our Lady MacTrump,
And no one in the manor can say what.   20

KELLEYANNE   The last I saw, her physical appearance
Suggested naught to kindle my concern.
She eats and does the modest chores she's giv'n.

PUCKABEE   She just, well . . .

KELLEYANNE   —She's just well.

PUCKABEE   —Nay, she is not.
She wanders half the night, with bureaus speaking.   25

KELLEYANNE   This morning, she address'd the cabinet.

ENOS   How is't a problem?

PUCKABEE   *[pointing to a piece of furniture:]* —'Twas this cabinet.

ENOS   Ah. 'Tis surprising.
KELLEYANNE   —And confusing, Doctor.
                  She speaks to teacups, paintings, chandeliers,
                  And takes her lunches with a shrubbery.   30
KELLEYANNE   What shall we do?
ENOS   —I know not! I am not
                  A doctor of the psyche. Why not ask
                  The neurosurgeon you do keep around.
PUCKABEE   That quack thinks Jesus kill'd the dinosaurs!
KELLEYANNE   Pray, Doctor, give us counsel.
ENOS   —First things first.   35
                  Where is the headcase?

          Enter LADY MACTRUMP *carrying a doublet and a candle.*

PUCKABEE   —Lo, e'en now she comes!
KELLEYANNE   This may be double-double trouble.
ENOS   —Hide!
                  [Puckabee, Kelleyanne, and Enos hide behind
                        the cabinet and watch Lady MacTrump.
LADY M.   *[to doublet:]* There is a frightful stain upon thy back.
                  A disappointing blot, I do confess—
                  Mayhap I could convince the populace   40
                  The marks were made by sitting in a chair,
                  Or leaning up against graffiti'd walls
                  So wet with paint that they did leave these strange
                  Impressions on the doublet. Verily,
                  If I foreknew the backlash I'd endure   45
                  When first I wrote the few words thereupon,
                  I'd ne'er have penn'd them. O, thou naughty doublet!
ENOS   God's wounds. The lady's daffy!

PUCKABEE   —Thou dost see!

ENOS   Hath she been ever thus?

KELLEYANNE   —I know but this:
She hath not slept since she and Lord MacTrump   50
Exchang'd their vows.

ENOS   —How long ago was that?

KELLEYANNE   'Twas sixteen years, and near as many months.
                              [Bells jingle.

ENOS   Hark, hark! I hear a tintinnabulation.

PUCKABEE   The jester comes. Be silent presently!

Bells jingle louder. Enter FOOLIANI.

FOOLIANI   Good even, sleepy lady.

LADY M.   *[to Fooliani:]*   —Noble knight,   55
I bid thee well. I prithee, honor me
By slaying the disorienting dragon
That hath encirclèd its confusing coils
Around my restless mind. I stainage see
Upon my garments, which doth speak to me   60
In ways that do make sleep impossible.
Inspect this doublet, please. What should I do?
And how remove th'embarrassment thereof?
                  [Fooliani examines the doublet.

FOOLIANI   Unless I am illiterate, it seems
There's writing hereupon.

LADY M.   —My hero, thou!   65
What doth it say, O noble man of letters?

FOOLIANI   It reads: "I verily don't care. Do you?"

LADY M.   *[to doublet:]* O, naughty spot that still is not rubb'd
                                out!

The tiny hands of migrant children e'en
Could not erase the blot. O, suffering!   70
Though I have scrubb'd, thy message still appears
And I do pay the cost. They think me heartless—
A simple and unthinking former model
And not a model lady. I'll not have't!
They say that FLOTUF hath a rotten motive.   75
No doublet may humiliate me so,
Especi'lly such an inexpensive one.
Be gone, foul stain. I'll make thee disappear,
For what I wrote now noisome turns for me!
                    [Exit Lady MacTrump.

FOOLIANI   Please do! I verily don't care as well.   80
                    [Fooliani shakes his marotte.
                    Bells jingle. Exit Fooliani.

KELLEYANNE   Is't safe enow for us to doublespeak?

ENOS   Indeed it must be—you must be first to hear
My carefully consider'd diagnosis:
The woman, speaking medic'lly, is crack'd.

PUCKABEE   What mounting madness! Her mind hath been riv'n.   85
Profoundest tragedy.

KELLEYANNE   —This may explain
Why she and Lord MacTrump have never made
The beast with double backs since they arriv'd
Into the White Hold.

ENOS   —Foh! Say, is there some
Nepenthe in this cab'net strong enow   90
To purge that horrid image from my pate?
                    [Enos attempts to open the cabinet.

PUCKABEE   Be still! We do not know if it is safe
For us to come forth from our hiding place.

KELLEYANNE   All seemeth safe; no clue of her I see.

PUCKABEE   Where hath our lady gone, so wondrous quick?   95

Enter FOOLIANI *from the cabinet.*

FOOLIANI   She's in the kitchen with the candlestick.
                [The others scream, startled. Fooliani
                shakes his marotte. Bells jingle. Exeunt.

SCENE 6.

In the White Hold dining hall.

Enter MACTRUMP *and* DAME DESDIVANKA.

MACTRUMP   Despite my lady's strange nocturnal walks,
               Of which the doctor telleth me of late,
               Methinks the day arriveth with new hope.
               Last night, I slumber'd better than I have
               This fortnight past—my bladder woke me not,   5
               My thoughts were settl'd calmly in my mind,
               And I awoke refresh'd for what may come.

DESDIVANKA   Your news is wondrous, Father, for I know
               Too long you have been plagu'd by lack of sleep.

MACTRUMP   For certain, some of it was for good reason.   10
               Let us enjoy a hearty feast together—
               'Tis well past lunchtime, and 'tis my desire
               To name you my new aide-de-camp whilst all

Are too stuff'd up with food to stand or speak.
Pray, summon all the chumps, the chaff, and chefs! 15
DESDIVANKA Yes, Father.

[Exit Desdivanka.
MACTRUMP —This shall be the best of times.
[*Calling:*] McTweet!

Enter MCTWEET.

McTWEET —You call'd a bird of finest feather?
MACTRUMP Tell me the latest news, McTweet.
McTWEET —It says:
[McTweet produces several pages
and reads from them.
Your newest judge for our esteem'd High Court
Hath waken'd faithful voters and hath giv'n 20
The Democrati multitude forebodings,
A thing MacTuttle thinks shall help him hold
The Northern Chamber in November next.
MACTRUMP A clever gambit. Please, send compliments
To Turtleneck.
[McTweet makes a note with his quill.
McTWEET —I shall! [*Reading:*] There was a rally 25
Across the river, which some tweeters fear
May violent become.
MACTRUMP —Why? Who is there?
McTWEET Some members of the neo Swastiklan
Withal Konfed'rate Knights of Khristendom.
MACTRUMP O, all good people, those. Do let me know 30
If any of them injur'd are.
McTWEET —Yea, lord.

Enter DONNISON *and* ERICSON.

DONNISON   My father!

MACTRUMP   —Issue! What brings ye to me?

DONNISON   We hither come with most perplexing news,
               Yet hope-fill'd, too.

ERICSON   —Which doth involve two ladies!

MACTRUMP   Two ladies, eh? Well, I should like to hear't!   35
               We are about to dine upon our luncheon.
               Shall you two join? The mess is bringing forth
               MacWhoppers, Chicken Niblets, and fillets;
               And we, of course, shall all have fries with that.

DONNISON   Delightful in the height! Yea, count us in.   40

MACTRUMP   Then we shall gladly toast the House MacTrump!
               I prithee, boys, hold back your news for last.
               I've vital news to share about your sister,
               And ye should be here when I do announce.

DONNISON   We'll heed your call and wait our cue.

ERICSON   —Hurrah!   45

McTWEET   My lord MacTrump, these final sheets detail
               Developments come from the inquisition.

MACTRUMP   I need not hear them now. Shoo! Buzz off, buzzard.
               May I not share a moment with my sons?

DONNISON   Yea! Beat it, birdbrain!

ERICSON   —Find a worm to chew!   50

McTWEET   [*aside:*] These apples did not fall far from their tree.
                             [*Exit McTweet.*

Enter DAME DESDIVANKA *and* LORD JARED KUSHREW.

DESDIVANKA   Wise Father, all your staff do stand assembl'd.

MacTRUMP	Good. Send them in.
DONNISON	—Fair greetings, family!

     [Kushrew waves. Desdivanka does not.

DESDIVANKA	O, boys, what errand brings you hither now?	
DONNISON	We have intelligence about our father,	55
	Which we learned from the protestors.	
ERICSON	—Two ladies!	
DESDIVANKA	But Father, sanction you their presence here?	
MacTRUMP	Of course! If they would play the part of grown-ups,	
	They shall be seated at the big boys' table.	
DESDIVANKA	As you desire, my lord and sovereign.	60

    [*Aside:*] A thousand poxes on my brothers two
    Should they disrupt this most important lunch!

Enter SIR JOHN MACKEELEY, LADY KELLEYANNE BOLEYN,
LADY SARAH PUCKABEE, SIR MICHAEL POMPEII,
and GUARDS *carrying trays of food.*

MacTRUMP	Be seated, ev'ryone, and tuck ye in!	
	[All sit and begin to eat.	
	As ye well know, there have been many changes	
	Within the White Hold since I took the throne.	65
	I stand most proud of some, while others prov'd	
	Disgraceful, sad, and fit for total losers.	
	'Tis wherefore I shall fire Sir John MacKeeley	
	As aide-de-camp and shall replace him with	
	My brilliant, lovely daughter, Desdivanka . . .	70
MacKEELEY	Wait, what?	
POMPEII	[*rising:*] —My lord MacTrump, I must object!	
MacTRUMP	Mayhap I shall appoint Lord Kushrew as	
	My new and loyal secret'ry of state	

	Anon since thou, Pompeii, so soon object'st.	
MacKEELEY	My lord MacTrump, if I may speak a word—	75
DESDIVANKA	Another word from thee and I shall make	
	My first achievement thine immediate	
	Discharge for insubordination. Tut!	
KELLEYANNE	This is so plusgood, lord, I speechless am.	
PUCKABEE	My lord, how shall I tell this to the public?	80
DESDIVANKA	Thou canst begin, thou Suckerbee, by showing	
	This most unworthy officer the door	
	And telling all thy mewling faux news cronies	
	The reason wherefore thou still hast a job.	
	Unless, of course, thou wishest to be fir'd.	85
MacTRUMP	[to sons:] Is not my daughter wonderful?	

                          [Donnison and Ericson look up
                             from their plates, with their mouths
                             too full of food to speak.

DONNISON	—Mff?
ERICSON	—Erg?
MacKEELEY	[to Desdivanka:] Speak not so boldly to me, nasty woman!
MacTRUMP	What? Nasty? Thou wouldst disrespect my daughter
	With that same word that I did use to outrage
	The Democrati fiend Hillaria? 90
MacKEELEY	You reek of mockery and monarchy.
	Enjoy your feast; MacMueller soon shall serve
	You all indictments for your just deserts!
DESDIVANKA	So bleat the sheep within MacMueller's flock.
	Have a MacLambchop as thou dost depart. 95

                  [Kushrew offers MacKeeley a sandwich.
                    MacKeeley throws it on the ground
                    and stomps on it. Exit MacKeeley.

MacTRUMP	This luncheon was a thrill. Doth anyone
	Have aught additional that they would speak?

Enter McTweet.

McTWEET	My lord, that protest I spake of before
	Hath lately, as was fear'd, turn'd violent!
	[*Reading:*] "The people gather'd silently this morn, 100
	The fog of early fall encircling them.
	A man enwrapp'd in flag confederate
	Approach'd the helpless protestors, as though
	He merely would discuss some point withal.
	When he drew closer, though, his purpose chang'd. 105
	More swiftly than a person can imagine,
	He drew his weapon, aim'd toward the crowd,
	And fir'd his gun incessantly thereon.
	The shooter had e'en better armor than
	The officer who fin'lly struck him down." 110
MacTRUMP	Ah. Too bad.
DONNISON	—Protest? Where?
McTWEET	—Across the river.
DESDIVANKA	What are the numbers like?
McTWEET	—Beg pardon?
ERICSON	—Ah!
DESDIVANKA	How many dead or hurt?
MacTRUMP	—Yea, make report.
	If small enow, we may not have to speak.
PUCKABEE	Which is less work for me, the heav'ns be thank'd. 115
McTWEET	A dozen citizens, at least, were injur'd,
	And two were kill'd. Two women, roommates both,
	Who have attended many peaceful protests,

	And both from families of immigrants—	
	One callèd Marianne and one Justine.	120
ERICSON	O Lord! Justine?	
DONNISON	—And Marianne? Alas!	
	How shall we bed them, if they have been slain?	
McTWEET	Four hundredth public shooting of the year.	
	As previously, victims were defenseless,	
	The killer proudly voted for MacTrump,	125
	And legislation shall not change a whit.	
	Republicons are sharing sympathies—	
	Should I send forth a message from you, too?	
MACTRUMP	Pray do. McTweet, please tell my followers	
	That House MacTrump sends out our thoughts and	
	pray'rs.	130
DESDIVANKA	Yet only if this first report is true—	
	If it is prov'n the two are persons real.	
MACTRUMP	Ah, yes. To err with caution, daughter dear,	
	Is wiser than to err with full support,	
	For I have heard intelligence of late	135
	Suggesting so-call'd victims of mass shootings,	
	Together with their so-call'd families,	
	May be but crisis actors on their stage,	
	Deliv'ring a performance worthy of	
	Dick Burbage when he wept as ancient Lear.	140
	[Donnison and Ericson look sadly at each other.	
	What is it, boys? Hath something made you ill?	
DONNISON	Of course we cannot certain be, and yet	
	Methinks these were no actors, they were real—	
	As real as we do stand before you now.	
ERICSON	These women two—Justine and Marianne—	145
	Are those selfsame to whom we lost our hearts.	

	Of course, the two were liberals and mean,	
	And would not give their love to us anon.	
DESDIVANKA	O, be not too sad, brothers—as you know,	
	The sea contains a school of fish.	
DONNISON	—Not so,	150
	We'd rather be with ladies sweet, not fish.	
ERICSON	And ne'er did I like school.	
DESDIVANKA	—Ye miss the point.	
	Besides, those trollops were not right for ye:	
	I gander'd by the blossoms as you two	
	Did hunt these wenches cheap like jungle cats.	155
	They shar'd obscenities about our father	
	And wish'd MacMueller would destroy our name!	
	You flew like flies unto the honeypot.	
MacTRUMP	Is't true? My sons, are these the women whom	
	You wish'd to tell me of? What fops you are.	160
	How oft have I told you not to engage	
	A lady 'less she hath already sign'd	
	Our family's strong nondisclosure contracts?	
DONNISON	Apologies, my sis and father both—	
	We had a momentary lapse of judgment,	165
	Which, thankfully, this slaying sets aright.	
ERICSON	These ladies were but primer for our pumps,	
	The op'ning act before the headliner,	
	The appetizer ere the entrée comes.	
	We'll find another, better set of ladies,	170
	Who do not hate our noble father so	
	And have not such foul notions in their brains.	
DONNISON	[to Ericson:] When ladies have ideas, what good can	
	follow?	
MacTRUMP	For my part, I shall never trust a lass	

	Who cultivates opinions by herself.	175
ERICSON	In troth, 'tis best t'avoid thought altogether.	
DONNISON	Well spoken, Ericson! Let our minds be	
	As empty as our pocketbooks are full.	
	This talking hath giv'n me an appetite:	
	Shall we to Hootersville, to get some wings	180
	And ogle all the waitresses therein?	
	Therein, all know and love our family!	
ERICSON	'Twill perfect be, thus to reset our hearts!	
MacTRUMP	Ha, ha, good boys!	
DESDIVANKA	—Ye aptly play your parts.	

                                        [Exeunt, laughing.

ACT
V

SCENE 1.

In the Oval Tower on the eve of the midterm election.

Enter CHORUS.

CHORUS   The scene turns tragic—heavy are our hearts—
             As liberty and justice fall to hate.
             November brings new actors to new parts,
             As forty Democrati demonstrate.
             MacTrump, in seeking favor with his base,   5
             Shall never rest until he hath his wall.
             Each place he passionately makes his case,
             First "build," then "finish" doth become the call.
             Shall he conclude the work that he began?
             And shall the staunch Republicons abet?   10
             Shall he fulfill the vows on which he ran?
             Or shall the Democrati block him yet?
             Our last act: harmony or revolution?
             Whate'er doth come, expect no resolution.
                                             [Exit Chorus.

Enter MacTRUMP, SENATOR MITCH MacTUTTLE,
and SENATOR GRIMSBY LINDSEYLOCKS.

MacTRUMP   [*to Lindseylocks:*] Close thou the door, I bid thee,
                                             Lindseylocks.   15
                        [Lindseylocks closes the door.
             Nay, close it with thee on the other side.
                                             [Exit Lindseylocks.

	[*To MacTuttle:*] I do not understand. Why is that imp	
	So kind to me of late? Why, verily,	
	Are any of you? Loathe we not each other?	
MacTUTTLE	'Tis known as solidarity, my lord.	20
	Th'election shall begin in sev'ral hours.	
	If we are not united, then we must	
	At least appear to be.	
MacTRUMP	—For whom? I do	
	Not owe thee favors, nay! 'Tis thou who shouldst	
	Bestow thy favor on MacTrump, for I—	25
	As though a pilot of a ship—do keep	
	Thy candidates afloat. Republicons	
	Like thee are wherefore I cannot construct	
	The wall my people want. Ye could not e'en	
	Destroy O'Bamacare. What is the matter?	30
	Dost thou propose to win through epic failure,	
	Or art thou just incompetence complete?	
MacTUTTLE	Yet, Master President, we're confident	
	We'll keep the Northern Chamber.	
MacTRUMP	—Confident?	
	We should be on the offense, barnacle!	35
	McTweet, come hither now!	

Enter McTweet.

McTWEET	—Good even, sir.
	How goes that migrant caravan you conjur'd?
MacTRUMP	Quit jesting, featherweight, and tell this turtle
	How we are faring in the Senate race.
McTWEET	One moment, please.
	[*McTweet shuffles through papers.*

MacTRUMP	—Be faster. How goes it?	40
McTWEET	Much like a dodo in a caucus race.	
MacTUTTLE	Methinks we'll capture some six Senate seats.	
McTWEET	According to the numbers I behold,	
	It shall be more like two or one.	
MacTUTTLE	—Thou'rt wrong.	
McTWEET	Art thou so sure? These pages came from thine	45
	Own canvassers. Seest thou the elephant?	

> [McTweet shows the pages to MacTuttle.
> Outraged, MacTuttle snatches them
> and stuffs them in his pocket.

MacTUTTLE	Lies, Master President—disgusting lies!	
McTWEET	[smiling:] O? What else have you got there in thy	
	pocket?	
MacTRUMP	Enow of this. What of the Southern Chamber—	
	Shall the Republicons still hold the House?	50
McTWEET	It doth depend. Is Prosperosi still	
	A staunch Republicon?	
MacTUTTLE	—Was she e'er?	
McTWEET	—Nay!	

> [Exit McTweet, laughing.

MacTRUMP	[to MacTuttle:] He did not even ask me for a tweet.	
	Know'st thou how awkward that doth make me seem?	
MacTUTTLE	Lord President MacTrump, as long as we	55
	Control the Northern Chamber, Prosperosi	
	Shall never have the pow'r to stop us from	
	Confirming judges popular withal	
	The party ranks.	
MacTRUMP	—What good will that do us	
	If, soon, our party cedes the Southern Chamber?	60
	Thou art far in above thy head, MacTwerp.	

Thy recklessness has galvaniz'd our foes!
My caddy could conduct the Northern Chamber
With far more skill than thee. If thou'rt not careful,
I may just fire thee!

MacTUTTLE   —Master President,   65
You do not have that pow'r.

MacTRUMP   —What didst thou say,
MacButthole?

MacTUTTLE   —Master President, there is
A separation of the pow'rs within
Our government for moments such as this.
You don't have the power to remove   70
Me from my post, though I maintain and wield
The power to remove you, sir, from yours.

MacTRUMP   Who sayeth so? Where is such nonsense written?

MacTUTTLE   The Constitution of th'United Fiefdoms.
In Article the First, in Section Three.   75
I have it here for reading, if you wish.

                          [MacTuttle pulls a copy of the
                              Constitution from his pocket.

MacTRUMP   Think'st thou dost pose a threat, vain turtledove?

MacTUTTLE   Make me not teach you suffering, MacTrump.
I am an expert in it—always was.
When I was but a child, a horrid sickness   80
Near robb'd me of the strength to use my legs.
My parents gave up all they own'd to save me.
It nearly ruin'd them. Behold me now.
Their sacrifices are what brought me here,
More powerful upon my feet than you   85
Behind your desk. Should Prosperosi seize
The Southern Chamber, then shall the decision

Of whether to remove you from this castle
And send you to MacMueller rest with me.
            [MacTuttle puts the Constitution in his pocket.
The Northern Chamber's mine, my lord, and all   90
Our senators would gladly vote for your
Removal and replacement with Lord Pound
In less time than it takes a man to nod.
So please, MacTrump, do try to think for once
About the enemies you're quick to make.   95

MacTRUMP   [*narrowing his eyes:*] Who told you this word?

MacTUTTLE   —What word?

MacTRUMP   —"Suffering"—
The interesting word thou didst employ.
Did someone order thee to speak the word?
It soundeth so familiar to mine ears.

MacTUTTLE   What do you mean by that?

MacTRUMP   —I think thou knowest   100
Exactly what I mean.

MacTUTTLE   —You are in jest.

MacTRUMP   Appear I like my jester Fooliani?
If thou think'st we must masquerade as friends,
Pray, tell me more about this suffering.

MacTUTTLE   What is this game you play?

MacTRUMP   —Nay, 'tis no game.   105
Tell me, MacTuttle, how it made thee feel
When thou didst lose the strength thou once enjoy'dst.

MacTUTTLE   I have no time for this.
                    [MacTuttle moves toward the doors.

MacTRUMP   —Guards!

Enter two GUARDS. *MacTuttle freezes.*

GUARD 1	—Yes, my lord?
MacTRUMP	My friend and I are planning to discuss
	His feeble legs. [*To MacTuttle:*] Wilt thou continue,

sir? 110

[*MacTuttle is speechless.*

I see. The frighten'd turtle must be shy.
Please, grant us privacy.

GUARD 2	—Yes, sovereign.

[*Exit guards.*

MacTRUMP	Thou'st serv'd in Washingtown for far too long,

Which warp'd thine eyesight like the slimy fishbowl
In which thou wert conceivèd. I know how　　　115
This swamptown works more than the senators
Thou dost surround thyself with; 'tis an act,
A silly circus where the sideshow freaks
Earn fraudulent election to the jobs
No one in their right mind would ever want.　　120
Thou hast no pow'r because no one desires
To be like thee. Thou hast no following,
No devotees, no soldiers. Thou couldst not
Fill up a rally held inside a shoebox.
Thou couldst not even hold O'Bama to　　　125
A single term. Why dost thou think I shall
Be easier? Toad, thou couldst not remove
Me if thou tried'st! Now ev'rything makes sense:
Thou art the reason why Putain told me
To make thy wife one of my secretaries.　　130
'Twas not so she would serve me, nay. It was
So she would have the might to serve me thee!

MacTUTTLE	Do not presume to speak of her again.
MacTRUMP	Who? Mine own minister of transportation?

O, foolish man, a child who reckons sums   135
Would have no trouble figuring your totals—
You both are losers, stuck in my employ!
If thou dost threaten me again, I'll call
MacMueller, thereupon to talk about
The strange behavior that my daughter notic'd   140
Betwixt thy wife and thine own Senate office
The moment she hath started working here.
I know of ev'ry wicked backdoor dealing
That thou and thy base wife do for thy contracts
Within thy backwoods, thistle-chewing fiefdom.   145
'Tis wherefore thou art such a knave, MacTuttle.
With thine experience, thou knowest how
To take on Democrati politicians,
But would not last one round against MacTrump.
An Army and a Navy I command,   150
With followers enow to conquer countries.
Pray tell, what dost thou have? A constitution?
If thy great constitution held true pow'r,
'Twould not have one like me defending it.

MacTUTTLE   Forgive me, sir, perhaps I did misspeak—   155

MacTRUMP   Nay, nay, methinks thou spakest candidly,
And now I finally do understand thee.
Be gone, and back to hell now, tattletale.
Thou hast a wall to build, with one or two
New senators to help thee do the task.   160
So get it done.

MacTUTTLE   —The Democrati won't
Allow you to construct your brazen wall.

MacTRUMP   Then it is well they're not in power yet.
The clock doth tick, MacTuttle—build my wall;

Or I shall close the government until　　　165
Thou dost.

MacTUTTLE　　　　　　　　—Yet, 'tis impossible! You can't
Construct your wall without the government,
Nor can I help if stripp'd of ev'ry power!

MacTRUMP　　Methought thou saidst thou wert the one in charge.
[*Smiling:*] Close thou the door upon thy swift way

out. 170

　　　　　[*Exit MacTuttle. MacTrump rises from his
　　　　　desk and walks to the center of the room.*
Ho, Gargamiller?

　　　Flash of light and puff of smoke.
　Enter GARGAMILLER *through the trapdoor.*

GARGAMILLER　　　　　　　—Fiery rose the angels,
And as they rose a vast, deep thunder roll'd!
　　　　　　　　　　[*Thunder. Lightning.*

MacTRUMP　　Pray, Gargamiller, tell it to me straight:
Dost thou have aught within your bag of tricks
That may help us secure the Southern Chamber?　175

GARGAMILLER　[*hissing:*] Pray, let me see.

　*Gargamiller takes a bag out of his cloak and shakes
　it open. Enter the trolls* BLACKFACE, COULTERGEIST,
　GERRYMANDER, *and* LA CUCARACHA *from the trapdoor.*

　　　　　　　　　　—'Tis all of them, my liege.

MacTRUMP　　Thou hast naught new for me?

GARGAMILLER　　　　　　　—Nay, lord and master.

MacTRUMP　　Then it appears that Prosperosi shall

Bring down her hammer to destroy my wall.

> [Gargamiller hisses. Exeunt
> Gargamiller with trolls.

Though I have shown my bluster to MacTuttle,   180
The truth is that my soul is sore afeard.
MacMueller cometh for me earnestly,
And if he comes I must have some defense—
The wall, as wall, is unimportant and—
I shall admit—unnecessary, too.   185
Yet as a symbol for my fervent base,
The wall's important as the air I breathe—
It is a battlement against my foes,
A rampart for the coming skirmishes,
The parapet on which MacTrump doth stand.   190
Should foul men come beseeching my impeachment,
I've need of citizens who shall demand
The rescue of their hero, e'en MacTrump:
The man who sav'd us from the coming hordes
By shoring up our frightful, southern border.   195
Mine ev'ry hope is built upon the wall,
It is my strength, my refuge, and my all.

> [Exit MacTrump.

SCENE 2.

*Desdivanka's fortress, Washingtown, on
the evening of the midterm election.*

Thunder. Raindrops. Enter DAME DESDIVANKA, *dressed in black,
stepping through a doorway to her bedroom patio. She turns
and faces a large wooden box atop a table in her bedroom—
the iObscura. The box has a thick cloak draped over it.*

DESDIVANKA   [*into iObscura, smiling:*] The greatest privilege of
being an
American is having your voice heard.
Get out and vote! Let not the rain stop you.

Enter McTWEET *from beneath the cloak.*

McTWEET   Brava, my mistress! And courageous, too,
Of thee to stand outside amid the drizzle!   5
DESDIVANKA   'Twas nothing. Shall we have another go?
McTWEET   There is no need. The iObscura captur'd
Each word and body motion utterly.
I am most grateful, damsel, for thy time!
         [*Desdivanka steps back into her bedroom,
         and McTweet closes the door behind her.*
DESDIVANKA   My thanks, and I would add some words as well.   10
McTWEET   Indeed—what shall be written?
         [*McTweet takes the quill from his cap.*
DESDIVANKA   —"VOTE, VOTE,
VOTE!"
         [*McTweet writes upon a parchment.*
McTWEET   Of course, the "V" and "O" thing. Duly noted!
DESDIVANKA   Now fly, thou bird. A tempest comes anon.
McTWEET   Indeed, she doth. [*Bowing:*] Be well. [*To offstage:*]
The lady's done!

Enter LORD JARED KUSHREW.

KUSHREW	Thanks, birdie! I pray thou dost know the exit?	15
McTWEET	I pray the lot of you will witness quite	
	The exodus tonight! I'll be the first.	

> *[McTweet takes the camera obscura
> and dons a cape. Exit McTweet.*

DESDIVANKA   Good husband.

KUSHREW   —Dearest princess!

DESDIVANKA   —Nay. Say empress.

KUSHREW   Forsooth. For thou art both my queen and country.

> *[They embrace.*

How goes the war?

DESDIVANKA   —About as splendid as   20
The weather.

KUSHREW   —Verily? Thou think'st it splendid?
I find this weather passing awful. No?

> *[Prolonged thunder and lightning.*

DESDIVANKA   I know. A tidal wave of blue hath grown
Across this nation many months. I hop'd
Our districts might outlast it, yet hope is   25
A worthless coinage when one banks on it.
Our allies on the Hill are frauds. They'll lose
The Southern Chamber, half a dozen seats
Within the Senate, and some gov'rnorships
We should have won.

KUSHREW   —If doom is in thy forecast,   30
Then wherefore dost thou seem at peace withal?

DESDIVANKA   [*laughing:*] My husband, hast forgotten who I am?
Nay, not at peace, yet utterly prepar'd
For what is next. I see the strategy

The simple Democrati shall employ: 35
They shall obstruct our lord with newfound strength,
Which is precisely what he needs to set
Himself apart from the Republicons
Who fall tonight. Let Prosperosi take
Her silly hammer to my father's wall.   40
Should she destroy it, Father's followers
Will have our Democrati foes to blame.
Do not forget: it would have taken years
To literally build my father's wall.
The plans alone would take us longer than   45
The law allows our presidents to serve.
By taking back the Southern Chamber and
Then making Father's wall a hopeless cause,
The Democrati fools will free us from
The burden of delivering the work!   50
This shall enrage my father's acolytes,
And he shall play them like an organist—
Pull out the stops on all their fear in time
For them to reelect him two years hence.
No adversary hath the strength to change   55
The outcome of a vote—not even foul
MacMueller, nor his base inquisitors.
The power of our people shall secure
My father's rule, and I shall run as his
Successor on the promise to complete   60
His mighty wall. O, yea, sweet husband, yea!
I see our pathway forward, lit with lights
That stretcheth from this bedroom to the distance:
The White Hold and the Oval Tower, mine!

[The two embrace and gaze
through the window.

KUSHREW   I see it too, my love! I see it plainly!   65
And with some luck, perhaps thy father's failures
Will damage the Republicons tonight
Beyond repair!
[Kushrew smiles. Desdivanka does not.
She awkwardly pats her husband.

DESDIVANKA   —'Tis right, my husband, yea.

KUSHREW   I cannot wait one minute more. McTweet!

Enter MCTWEET *from the balcony,*
wearing a cloak drenched with rain.

McTWEET   I bid a second blessing to you both.   70
Apologies for my most sodden state.

KUSHREW   Think nothing of it. Prithee, speak to us
About the parliamentary elections.
How do the Democrati fare?

McTWEET   —One moment.
[McTweet consults his parchments.

DESDIVANKA   Hath Prosperosi won the Southern Chamber?   75

McTWEET   According to my readings, she hath not.

DESDIVANKA   Indeed?

KUSHREW   —In sooth?

McTWEET   —Just as I spake! Nay. Wait.
[McTweet unfurls the scroll.
Most sorry—I did view the Pox Network,
Which hardly shall admit the night's results.
In faith, the Democrati took the chamber,   80
And Lady Prosperosi did just speak!

	She said: "Tonight historic victory
	Is in our grasp. This mighty victory
	We did not seek for our own party's sake,
	But for America's hardworking fam'lies." 85
KUSHREW	O, dearest love, methinks she spake of us!
DESDIVANKA	I think not. Mayhap thou shouldst go to bed,
	Kind husband. It appears I still have work
	To do tonight.
KUSHREW	—If thou insist'st. Rest well!

           [Kushrew kisses her and then
                     exits toward the bed.

McTWEET   *[to Desdivanka:]* My lady, there is still another
                                         speaker 90
         Who's trending at the moment. Wouldst thou like
         To watch her?

DESDIVANKA   —Possibly. Who is she, bird?

McTWEET   One Cleosandria O'Cassio,
         The new-elected congresswoman of
         Both Queensland and the Bronxford in New
                                     Yorktown. 95
         She is the youngest woman e'er elected
         Unto the Southern Chamber!

DESDIVANKA   —Yea? I would
         Observe her speech.

McTWEET   —Hast thou a mirror black?

DESDIVANKA   Upon the wall there. Why?

McTWEET   —The feed is streaming.

         [McTweet pulls out a vial of shiny liquid from
          his cloak. Desdivanka takes it. Exit McTweet
           to growing thunder. Desdivanka hurries to
            her mirror, uncorks the vial, and drinks its

liquid. She then stares into the black mirror.
The room darkens. Smoke rises. The sound
of cheers and clapping fills the room.

Enter CLEOSANDRIA O'CASSIO *above, on balcony,*
dressed in white, with a CROWD *watching her.*

O'CASSIO We have made history tonight, my friends— 100
The youngest woman serving Parliament.
'Tis what is possible when people come
Together in collective realization
That all our actions, whether small or large,
Are capable of making lasting change. 105
    [Desdivanka steps closer towards the mirror.
   Her expression changes from curiosity to horror.
    As the crowd cheers louder, lightning flashes.
When people talk about the strong pursuit
Of our more perfect union, that, itself,
Commandeth us to progress as a nation,
To better grow and better be, as well.
Right now, our nation's on a crookèd path, 110
Yet 'tis our time to make the crookèd straight.
    [A roll of thunder shakes the bedroom,
      and Desdivanka makes a fist.
They'll ever call ambitious folk naive.
They'll say we're uninform'd and radical,
For we would change the country's power balance.
We'll fight to put more power in the hands 115
Of working, ev'ryday Americans—
Which is, methinks, where truly it belongs.

[Hatred washes over Desdivanka's
face. The vial breaks in her hand.
I am most proud to stand, shoulder to shoulder,
With ye in this most worthy, vital fight.
Today, friends, is our milestone, verily   120
'Tis a beginning—only the beginning.
[O'Cassio's audience breaks into
applause. They chant her name. Thunder
and lightning. Desdivanka screams.
Exeunt O'Cassio and crowd.

DESDIVANKA   Fie! Fie! A thousand curses on the wench!

DESDIVANKA *punches the mirror, smashing it*
to pieces. Enter LORD JARED KUSHREW.

KUSHREW   Is aught amiss, mine empress?
DESDIVANKA   —Get thee out!
[Exit Kushrew.

DESDIVANKA   The future rears its ugly, fearsome face—
One who may yet unite the people like   125
O'Bama with his messages of hope,
And "Yea we can!"—'tis hubris in the height!
The people, though, respond to promises
Of freedom, progress, liberty, and justice
Like sailors to a waiting siren's call.   130
It makes me sick, for peasants do not know
What's best for them—'tis wherefore they fear us.
These whining, stooping liberals would give
Their pitiful supporters far more pow'r
Than any ordinary, middle-class,   135
Uneducated plebeian should have.

O, how it makes my insides burn with hate
At peons gaining pow'r instead of me—
Of House MacTrump—who surely doth deserve't.
I'll rule the Democrati like a queen.   140
My father still hath power over all,
And we shall grind their system to halt.
We'll pull the precious government they would
Reclaim from out beneath their worthless feet.
Were there a hundred years of history,   145
No upstart fiend shall get the best of me.

> *[Exit.*

SCENE 3.

Atop the Oval Tower.

Enter MacTrump *above with* Viceroy Michael Pound, Lady Sarah
Puckabee, Lady Kelleyanne Boleyn, *and* guards. *They turn their
attention to* Lady Nancy Prosperosi, *below, who enters Parliament to
the applause of Republicon and Democrati* parliamentarians. *Among
them is the recently elected* Cleosandria O'Cassio. Prosperosi
waves and ascends the speaker's rostrum, where Speaker Pryam, *a boy
roughly ten or twelve years old, struggles to lift the wooden gavel.*

PROSPEROSI   [*to Pryam:*] Thou canst that keep. I have brought
                                   mine own hammer.
                 *[Prosperosi raises a warhammer from her
                 robes. The Democrati erupt in cheers.*

MᴀᴄTRUMP	That damnèd hammer of hers I can see
	From here. 'Tis most unfair. Why doth she have
	A hammer while I've none? I'm president!
	I should be deck'd in armor, as she is. 5
PUCKABEE	You do command the strongest military
	In all the world, my lord.
MᴀᴄTRUMP	—Yet if I hold
	No hammer yuge as hers, what good is it?
	I feel as impotent as I am mad.
	[Exeunt parliamentarians below.
	All right. The party's over. Back inside. 10
	[Everyone descends the turret and
	enters the interior of the Oval
	Tower below. Exeunt guards.
	What have we on the docket for today?
	How shall you losers help me build my wall?
KELLEYANNE	My lord, methinks we have a plusgood answer.
MᴀᴄTRUMP	I'll gladly hear't.
PUCKABEE	—With Lady Prosperosi
	And all the Democrati back in pow'r, 15
	We cannot hope to have the funds we need
	To build the mighty wall that you desire.
MᴀᴄTRUMP	No wall? This doth not start as I had hop'd.
PUCKABEE	Pray, listen on. You may yet compromise—
	They'll give you some concessions on the wall, 20
	Though not the billions for which you do ask,
	And in the bargain thou shalt fully fund
	The government, and thus avoid a shutdown.
	You shall be seen as generous and fair,
	A statesman at the apex of his might. 25
MᴀᴄTRUMP	What of the wall? What shall my base think of it?

KELLEYANNE   Sir, they shall think whate'er we tell them to.
               No follower of yours shall ever check
               To see if there is verily a wall.
               If we tell them the wall is near complete,   30
               They shall believe it.

MacTRUMP   —Truly?

KELLEYANNE   —By my troth.
                          [Pound produces a sheet of paper.

POUND   We have here, sir, the bill that you must sign
               To fund the government, avoid the shutdown,
               And make this plan of ours reality.
               Today, when Lady Prosperosi doth   35
               Arrive, with Charles Soother at her side,
               You shall surprise them both by giving them
               The very thing they seek of you—'twill shock
               Them, make them grateful. They shall owe you much.

MacTRUMP   Doth this plan have the blessing of my daughter   40
               And finest aide-de-camp, Dame Desdivanka?
                          *[Puckabee, Kelleyanne, and Pound
                             glance nervously at each other.*

KELLEYANNE   I double-doublethink it doth indeed?

MacTRUMP   Then I shall do it. Ye advise me well.
               Fetch me a quill that I may make it so.
                          *[Puckabee, Kelleyanne, and Pound
                             breathe a sigh of relief. Puckabee
                             hands MacTrump a quill.*

               Enter DAME DESDIVANKA.

DESDIVANKA   Cease all this pageantry! Bestill thy pen!   45
               I hope for all your sakes the ink is out

	So that our liege not strike it through your names!
MᴀᴄTRUMP	Sweet daughter, why so serious? This plan—

[Desdivanka stares at the others coldly.

DESDIVANKA   What plan?

MᴀᴄTRUMP   —To fund the government anon,

Make compromise to gain a partial wall,   50

But tell it to the public an 'twere whole.

DESDIVANKA   *[to Puckabee, Kelleyanne, and Pound:]* Yield.

[Exeunt Puckabee, Kelleyanne,
                                  and Pound hastily.

[To MacTrump:]   —Set the feather down;
                                   we need it not.

MᴀᴄTRUMP   This plan was not devis'd by thee, my pet?

DESDIVANKA   O Father, you have sorely been abus'd!

If ever I present you with a plan   55

That maketh you look ignorant and weak,

And setteth our cause backward many months,

You may declare me nevermore your child.

MᴀᴄTRUMP   It could not be!

DESDIVANKA   —A shutdown must commence.

To do so carefully shall demonstrate   60

That you alone do hold the winning cards.

The Democrati jacks in Parliament

Shall find themselves both weak and ill-prepar'd.

MacMueller, who may think he holds the ace,

Shall have no choice but forfeit all his chips—   65

The stakes shall rise above his finances.

Vile Prosperosi and her puppet Soother—

As rank a pair of jokers e'er there was—

Shall find themselves in a prolong'd debate

About the wall, which shall but work them woe.   70

They'll dig themselves a ditch with their own spades
Whilst you do capture all your foll'wers' hearts.
Hold 'em with words as strong as any club,
And harvest mines of diamonds 'mongst your base.
Then let the game go on for weeks or months—   75
The shutdown never ending, peradventure—
Each passing day your pow'r shall grow, employing
Exec'tive orders, taking ev'ry trick.
You'll bring them down an 'twere a house of cards—
MacTrump doth hold the trump card. Do you see?   80

MacTRUMP   Forsooth! Thou art my greatest counselor.
How shall I play the hand, when they arrive?

DESDIVANKA   Appear to be both generous and kind.
This pitfall, though, avoid: let them not put
The burden of the shutdown on your shoulders.   85
The fault must be upon the Democrati,
Or this strange beast may turn around and bite.
You must be ruthless as the lion and
As clever as the fox for this to work.
Does that make sense?

MacTRUMP   —Inherently, my dear.   90
When they arrive, I shall be naught but smiles,
And no responsibility assume
For shutting down the government anon.
Meanwhile, what of this bill they'd have me sign?
                [*Desdivanka holds the paper over a*
                    candle until it burns completely.

DESDIVANKA   Would that the paper were your enemies,   95
Each of them disappearing into smoke.
                [*There is a knock at the door.*

MacTRUMP   What is't?

Enter GUARD.

GUARD   —My sov'reign, Viceroy Pound withal
                The Democrati leaders is come hither.

MacTRUMP   We are prepar'd! Pray, send them in at once.

                                        [Exit Guard.

Enter LADY NANCY PROSPEROSI, SENATOR CHARLES
SOOTHER, *and* VICEROY MICHAEL POUND.

MacTRUMP   [*smiling:*] My viceroy Pound, come in. And Cryin'
                                        Chuck, 100
                How nice of you to join us.

SOOTHER   —Lord MacTrump.
                                [They shake hands.
                My thanks for giving us a reason to
                Shed tears of joy this past November, sir.

MacTRUMP   We won the Senate, Chuck. Is that not so?

SOOTHER   When one doth brag o'er winning North Dakastor 105
                And Indriana, too—both fiefdoms with
                Immense Republicon support—methinks
                One is in trouble.

MacTRUMP   [*smiling:*]   —Yet we won both, nay?
                And little Nancy—

PROSPEROSI   [*correcting:*]   —Madam Speaker, sir.
                        *[MacTrump tries to embrace her, but she
                        sits on a sofa and sets her hammer down.
                        It hits the floor with a loud, metallic
                        thud. Everyone sits except Desdivanka,
                        who slowly paces in the background.*
                Thanks for this meeting, Master President.   110

MACTRUMP	[*smiling:*] 'Tis not a problem, Nancy. Thanks for coming.
SOOTHER	We would discuss the spending bill with you.
MACTRUMP	[*smiling:*] I rather would discuss my needed wall, For which I do require the funds forthwith.
PROSPEROSI	Must you retreat so quickly to your wall? 115
SOOTHER	Sir, we had hop'd to speak of compromise.
MACTRUMP	[*smiling:*] I'll gladly compromise, once I have all That I desire.
PROSPEROSI	—Nay, 'tis no compact, sir.
MACTRUMP	[*smiling:*] What ever meanest thou, Miss Nancy? Hmm?
SOOTHER	I'm sure that you agree, sir, that the workers 120 Within the government deserve far better.
MACTRUMP	[*smiling:*] They do deserve their safety, which I shall Deliver to them in the form of wall.
PROSPEROSI	Are you in jest? We must be serious If we'd avoid the Shutdown of MacTrump. 125
	[Pause. MacTrump is shocked. Viceroy Pound sits silently, with eyes half shut.
MACTRUMP	What didst thou say?
SOOTHER	—Pray, Master President.
MACTRUMP	"The Shutdown of MacTrump"—those were thy words?
DESDIVANKA	[*aside:*] Nay, Father, stop—you wander from the script!
PROSPEROSI	You seem to be hell-bent on shutting down The government, which shall fore'er be known 130 In hist'ry as the Shutdown of MacTrump. 'Tis your responsibility—none other.
SOOTHER	We must have compromise to move past this—

	Our hands are tied if you demand the wall.	
MACTRUMP	If I get not what I desire, one way	135

MACTRUMP   If I get not what I desire, one way   135
Or th'other—whether 'tis through you, or through
A military action—yea, I shall
Shut down the government. In fact, I'm proud
To shut it all down for the sake of border
Security, Chuck. People do not want
The criminals and fiends hyp'd up on drugs   140
To pour into our country like a fountain.

DESDIVANKA   [*aside:*] Nay, Father, nay—this outcome is disastrous.
Thou shouldst frame Democrati, not take blame!

PROSPEROSI   Then let the Shutdown of MacTrump commence.

SOOTHER   [*smiling:*] Yea, let it. Thank you for your time, my
                                                                 liege. 145

MACTRUMP   Out! Out with ye! I'll shut it down with glee!
                    [*Confusion. Exeunt all except Desdivanka*
                                as MacTrump blusters off.

DESDIVANKA   He had one job—a stupid, simple task—
Let not a jot of blame fall on his shoulders
For shutting down the UF government.
Instead, what doth the bulging blockhead do?   150
He took the Democrati bait so quickly,
As if he were an undernourish'd shrimp.
Fie! Idiot to be so quickly foil'd.
I cannot count on him to lift me up;
By clinging to his coattails, I'll but fall.   155
A new path I must find, make my own way—
Break with my father's bumbling and dishonor
And find a wiser tyrant to embrace,
Perchance in Prussia or in North Korasia,
Where I shall despotism purely see   160

Without the base mix of hypocrisy.

[Exit.

SCENE 4.

In the Southern Chamber of Parliament.

Enter CLEOSANDRIA O'CASSIO.

O'CASSIO   The sound of throngs approaching pricks mine ears,
And sets my heart to beat in time with theirs.
Most fortunately, 'tis my kind of beat,
A rapid rise doth make for nimble feet.
                    [O'Cassio spins and dances briefly.
The people are enrag'd at both the parties   5
For failing to avoid this shutdown base,
A mockery of our democracy
That makes our government a laughingstock
To other nations all across the globe.
Indeed, there's only Brexeunt that's worse.   10
A portion of my colleagues are afeard—
They hear the din approaching, and have lock'd
Themselves away inside their offices,
As if they could ignore the sea of troubles,
And, by opposing, end them. Nay, not I—   15
The people must be seen, respected, heard.
No politician is above the people,
No height of office too beyond their reach,

No ear may be protected from their voice,
No representative above reproach,   20
Or else we have not serv'd our purpose here.
'Tis well I'm young; to win this fight will take
A generation more than many live.

She ventures into the hall. Enter LADY NANCY PROSPEROSI.

PROSPEROSI	My lady Cleosandria, well met.
	Hast heard the chanting of the coming throng? 25
O'CASSIO	Indeed! It seems the people would be heard,
	And I have come to meet them willfully.
PROSPEROSI	Thou holdest insight far beyond thy years—
	Yet twenty-nine but wiser than your elders.
O'CASSIO	My thanks. These words fall gently on mine ears, 30
	For thou hast ever been a paradigm,
	Though I could wish for someone younger to
	Be Speaker of the House.
PROSPEROSI	—Experience
	I proffer, far beyond what others bring.
O'CASSIO	Yet thou dismiss'st the Green New Deal too soon. 35
PROSPEROSI	Too soon? My dear, I have been fighting for
	The principles in thy proposal e'er!
	Votes I have cast protecting species whole
	From their extinction ere thou e'en wert born.
	This war I've vigorously fought for decades, 40
	Ascending past our hist'ry's other women
	Despite relentless ridicule from the
	Republicons and boors in our own party.
O'CASSIO	Please take my few critiques not as indiff'rence
	To thine achievements, Lady Prosperosi. 45

> The barriers you overcame are still
> A vicious cancer 'mongst the Democrati
> Despite thy years of trusted leadership.

PROSPEROSI If such blunt statements are thy best defenses,
               I'll wager that thou needest better weapons.   50
               Republicons already work against thee,
               And I'll not have thy fresh career disrupt
               Our party's goals, though thou art popular.
               Thou art a champion of change, my sister,
               And shalt earn for thyself a mighty hammer.   55
               Enthusiasm, though, is not enow
               To make thy greenest dreams realities.
               Yet if we would create change for the planet,
               We must needs be as subtle as the tides.

O'CASSIO Methinks the tides of change will sweep thee under   60
               Unless thou walk'st in step withal the times.
               For now, though, may we set aside these quarrels?
               The chanting crowd hath enter'd to the chamber—
               I prithee, wilt thou thither walk with me?

PROSPEROSI Yea, such was my intention. Let us go.   65

They walk through the halls. Enter a crowd of PROTESTORS.

PROTESTORS [*chanting:*] Something is rotten inside of this dump!
               Pay all the workers and furlough MacTrump!
               Stop the shutdown!
                       [*Protestors spot O'Cassio and Prosperosi.*

PROTESTOR 1 Behold, employees of the government
               Who still receive their recompense, e'en whilst   70
               Eight hundred thousand of our citizens
               Go sans a paycheck ev'ry fortnight. Shame!

PROTESTOR 2   Is this America? How can this be—
                The richest nation in the world entire
                Unable to pay workers for their toil.   75
O'CASSIO   Friends, people, citizens, lend me your ears:
                To shut down government is not the norm
                When politicians get not what we want.
                The truth of this vile shutdown, friends, is that
                'Tis actually not about a wall.   80
                The truth is worse: this shutdown is about
                The swift erosion of democracy,
                Subversion of our governmental norms,
                Which are most basic for our operations.
PROTESTOR 3   We love thee—Cleosandria ascendant!   85
PROTESTOR 4   [to Properosi:] Thou show'd the president a lion's
                                                    strength
                As thou negotiated over this—
                For that, thou hast our humble gratitude.
                What, though, shalt thou do next to force his hand?
PROSPEROSI   The Constitution calls the president   90
                From time to time to give unto both chambers
                Intelligence of the State of the Union.
                Alas, the UF Secret Servers and
                Department of UF Security
                Have not been funded twenty-six full days—   95
                With critical departments cut by furloughs.
                Thus, given the security concerns
                And, 'less the government doth open soon,
                We must determine dates alternative
                For President MacTrump to come deliver   100
                The State of th'Union. Let me be most clear:
                The Southern Chamber shall not take a vote

	To authorize the president's address
	Within the walls of our dear chamber if
	The government hath not been open'd. Yea: 105
	He hath no invitation to this house.
PROTESTOR 4	Three cheers for Prosperosi!
PROTESTORS	—Yea, hurrah!

They continue to chant. Enter MacTRUMP
and FOOLIANI *above, on balcony.*

MacTRUMP	She cannot disinvite me!
FOOLIANI	—Zounds, she can.
MacTRUMP	There must be aught that I can do!
FOOLIANI	—There's not.
MacTRUMP	Not one?
FOOLIANI	—You could be the first president 110
	To give the great address from Tow'r MacTrump.
MacTRUMP	Nay, it must be the Southern Chamber—fie!
	The queen hath trapp'd the king and call'd it 'mate.
	Yet, as I have whenever I have lost,
	I'll topple o'er the board and scatter pieces 115
	Across the room. I do not like to lose.
FOOLIANI	Then thou must have your cake and eat it, too—
	Beneficently ope the government,
	Then find another means to get your wall—
	For wall is good and wall is necessary. 120
MacTRUMP	Another means? I'll hear thee speak more on't.
	[Exeunt MacTrump and Fooliani from balcony.
O'CASSIO	Each member of this body hath a vast
	Responsibility unto this nation,
	To ev'ryone in the United Fiefdoms,

Yea, whether they did vote for us or not.   125
MacTrump shares that responsibility,
Which means he must needs answer unto ye.
                    [Exeunt O'Cassio and Prosperosi, waving.

PROTESTORS   Huzzah!
PROTESTOR 1   —The government must open'd be!
PROTESTOR 2   Eight hundred thousand need what they deserve!
                                        [All cheer.

PROTESTOR 1   Let us unto the Northern Chamber next!   130

                    Enter McTWEET *and* FOOLIANI, *aside.*

McTWEET   *[aside to Fooliani:]* Art thou most sure MacTrump
                                        would this proclaim?
                    The shutdown talk doth generate much traffic.
FOOLIANI   Forsooth! This next announcement shall be his
                    Late Christmas gift unto our citizens.
McTWEET   If thou art sure. *[To all:]* Such news you'll not believe! 135
                    The shutdown hath been ended by MacTrump,
                    Who reach'd agreement with the legislators
                    And shall soon sign a bill to open up
                    The government upon tomorrow's dawn.
                    It seems the time requir'd to break MacTrump   140
                    Is five-and-thirty days.
PROTESTORS   —Hurrah, at last!

                    Enter MacTRUMP *above, on balcony.*
                    All below listen intently.

MacTRUMP   Emergency! Emergency, I say!
                    Declare a national emergency!

McTWEET   [*aside:*] MacTrump: he is the gift that keeps on giving.

MACTRUMP   We'll have ourselves a great emergency,   145
The greatest, best emergency e'er known—
This 'mergency, I say, shall be so yuge.
There's an invasion of our country, see,
With drugs, with human traffickers, and such,
With ev'ry type of criminal and gang.   150
Of course, I did not need to do this thing—
I will that it be faster done, 'tis all.
I'll have emergency, and then have wall.

> [*The protestors yell angrily. Fooliani shakes*
> *his marotte. Bells jingle. All exeunt.*

SCENE 5.

The White Hold residence. Evening.

Enter GARGAMILLER *above the rooftop.*
It is snowing. An enormous red moon rises.

GARGAMILLER   The polar vortex swirleth round about,
And all of Washingtown is frightf'lly cold.
The planet's equilibrium upset,
The whole world teeters on a knife blade's edge.
Arising o'er the chill of winter's bite,   5
Behold! The blood wolf dragon moon ascends;
The fullest, reddest, most myster'ous orb
That we shall, in our lives, expect to see.

Like the eclipse that shock'd the nation so,
This messenger of heaven doth portend   10
A future whose events we may but guess!

                                           [*Exit Gargamiller.*

Enter MacTRUMP, LADY MacTRUMP, DAME DESDIVANKA, LORD
JARED KUSHREW, DONNISON, *and* ERICSON *in the family sitting room.*
A crackling fire fills the fireplace. MacTRUMP *paces impatiently.* LADY
MacTRUMP *peeks outside through window curtains.* DESDIVANKA
and KUSHREW *sit on a sofa, their eyes downcast.* DONNISON
and ERICSON *chat quietly and smoke cigars. Everyone is dressed*
for travel except the brothers, who are dressed for hunting.

MacTRUMP   I well know what I do—was born for this.
                So good am I. Amazing just how good.
                To use a national emergency
                To build my wall shall ever be known as   15
                The smartest act a president has done.
                They'll carve my face upon the mountains by
                The time I'm finish'd with this work. Yuge mountains.
                By heav'n, I could begin the work myself
                Once my great wall is built.

                                           [*A clock strikes.*
                                    —God damn the time!   20
                What takes the coachman so long to depart?
                Guard!

                        Enter GUARD.

GUARD   —Yes, my lord.
MacTRUMP   —Where are our carriages?

	I must to Mar-Iago presently	
	For greatly needed rest and relaxation.	
	My children, too, would go their sep'rate ways,	25
	Since we have some intelligence receiv'd	
	Of an unwelcome visitor who cometh.	
GUARD	Apologies, sire, but the weather is	
	Too foul for travel still. We must needs wait	
	Until the winter storm is past.	
MacTRUMP	—Forsooth,	30
	Thou art as useless as a Bible in	
	A whorehouse. Get thee out!	

[Exit Guard.

          —I cannot stand
This cursèd city and its lazy losers.
How else am I suppos'd to pass the time?

DESDIVANKA	Why not try reading something, father mine?	35
MacTRUMP	Art thou in jest? Hast thou observ'd the papers	
	With trait'rous LaCöhen on ev'ry page,	
	Dispensing lies about me for the world?	
	I need the comfort of my greens and holes.	
	Exertions lately have exhausted me—	40
	'Twas hard enough to find my Prussian passport	
	Inside a draw'r of presidential socks.	
	'Tis taxing.	
LADY M.	[*looking out the window:*] —Horrid more than taxes	
	due—	
	A red moon rises, and then disappears!	
	What is the portent thereof? Who can tell't?	45
	And wherefore noticeth no one but me?	
MacTRUMP	Tut! I care not for lunar lunatics.	

KUSHREW   [*to Desdivanka:*] Mine empress, shall I give her
                                       aught of comfort?

DESDIVANKA   Leave her unto her worries, gentle husband.
                  Good Doctor Enos recommends a trip   50
                  To cure her empty head of silly shame.

LADY M.   Ah yes, the Enos doctor told me that!
                  His soothing presence hath so help'd my mind—
                  Which, as you know, hath lately bother'd been—
                  That I shall gladly heed his keen advice.   55

MᴀᴄTRUMP   That's right, to Mar-Iago we must go,
                  Though I'd prefer my lovely daughter there.

DESDIVANKA   You have my fond affections, father-lord,
                  And overwhelming love and loyalty,
                  Yet, as you know, Lord Kushrew and myself   60
                  Must make our own adventure speedily.

MᴀᴄTRUMP   And whither are ye bound?

KUSHREW   —To North Korasia.

MᴀᴄTRUMP   What?
                       [*Desdivanka glares at Kushrew.*

DESDIVANKA   —Faith, we two shall meet with King John Ill.

KUSHREW   The man hath much to teach of leadership.

MᴀᴄTRUMP   'Tis true enow. At least, within his country,   65
                  He doth not have to live with criticism.
                  [*To Desdivanka:*] O, sweet one, prithee be thou not
                                       asham'd
                  That thou wouldst go see King John Ill sans me.
                  Thy strong ambitions know no height nor bound;
                  I would do likewise, were I in thy place.   70

DESDIVANKA   Most humble thanks.

MᴀᴄTRUMP   —And trav'lling mercies, too.

                       [*To Donnison and Ericson:*] Now, boys, I see ye are
                                             in gear array'd?

                       Bound are ye for another hunting trip?

DONNISON   Indeed we are!

MacTRUMP   —Yea, 'tis the spirit, sons!

                       Your trip, I'll wager, shall make you forget   75
                       The Democrati wenches e'er existed.

KUSHREW   How did this trip of yours arise, my bros?

DESDIVANKA   I gave them both a choice: a trip, or exile
                       With their half sister, trifling Tiffanay.

                       [*Aside:*] How I do wish they'd pick'd the other course   80
                       And chosen exile to some distant land.
                       I cannot get them far enow away.

KUSHREW   Do share, then—whither shall ye go, my chums?

MacTRUMP   Upon safari, there to kill some rhinos.

KUSHREW   Are they not found atop th'endanger'd list?   85

DONNISON   Yea, which is half the fun!

ERICSON   —'Tis why it's sport.
                       'Twould be too easy shooting common beasts.

DONNISON   I do confess great stirrings of excitement.

ERICSON   Wait 'til thou view'st the blunderbuss I've brought.

DONNISON   Hoo hoo! The hunt!

ERICSON   —We're on the prowl again!   90

MacTRUMP   All your expenses paid by mine accounts—
                       A price too small to see ye so engag'd.

                                       [*A clock strikes.*
                       God's wounds. Again? Are we to never leave?

                             Enter GUARD.

MacTRUMP   At last! I thought the coach would never come.

| | Do I have time to whiz before our flight? | 95 |

GUARD   My Lord, Sir Robert of MacMueller knocks.

MacTRUMP   Hie quickly to the secret passages!

[All exeunt in haste.

Enter SIR ROBERT OF MACMUELLER.

MacMUELLER   How inquisition tires the human soul!
               I, verily, deserve a holiday.
               Great numbers of those in the circle of   100
               His grace—the president—were in my sights,
               Cut down withal indictment and arrest.
               Recall I when MacTrump did fire Dogcomey—
               It made the Deaf Beehive his enemy.
               Months later, I may say it's been an honor   105
               Endeav'ring to discover truth through my
               Stern inquisition into Prussian meddling.
               And now, my body and my weary spirit
               Need time to mend for what I just have done—
               Delivering my last analysis.   110
               My last report unto Attorney Bardolph
               I've handed over, finishing my quest.
               Soon unto normal life I shall return,
               Delaying not a minute more than needed.
               Eyes ever on my back, harsh scrutiny—   115
               My work upon this case I shall not miss.
               Ere I depart, I've one last message, though,
               A special note for President MacTrump.
               Now that my obligation I've fulfill'd
               On such a public, vital case, I shall   120
               Relieve the burden of my conscience and

Send him a message I do hope he'll heed.

Enter MACTRUMP, LADY MACTRUMP, DESDIVANKA,
LORD JARED KUSHREW, DONNISON, *and* ERICSON
above, on balcony, watching MACMUELLER.

MACTRUMP	Canst see him? What is it he doth below?
DESDIVANKA	He doth approach the door below us.
MACTRUMP	—Why?

Would he, a single soldier, storm the White Hold?   125
What villainy is this the man doth ply?

ERICSON	It seems he hath some satchel on his back.
DONNISON	Dost think he's hither brought the whole report?
LADY M.	Alack, the moon hath sent its vicious hound!

          [MacMueller begins nailing a piece of
          paper to the door of the White Hold.

DESDIVANKA	It seems he posteth something on the door, 130

As if the White Hold were a noticeboard.

KUSHREW	Has his report fit into so few pages?

Methinks such summary is foolishness.

ERICSON	O Father, I'm afeard!

          [Ericson begins sucking his thumb.

MACTRUMP	—What's writ thereon?
KUSHREW	'Tis difficult to read from such a distance. 135

I wish I had not star'd at the eclipse.

          [Donnison pulls out the binoculars from
          his hunting gear and looks through them.

DONNISON	Here! These shall help me read the message, Father.

The missive seems innocuous enow;
A small request is written thereupon—
It seems he'd have you sign some file again.   140

DESDIVANKA   What? Give me that, thou dismal-dreaming lout!
                              [She snatches the binoculars from
                              Donnison and looks through them.

MACTRUMP   What seest? Is it hostile or benign?

DESDIVANKA   O, Father, steel your heart. It reads: "RESIGN."
                              [MacMueller picks up his satchel, prepares
                              to leave, and then looks over his shoulder
                              toward the balcony. The MacTrump
                              family ducks quickly. Exeunt omnes.

EPILOGUE.

Enter McTweet.

McTWEET For now, our curtain sets upon the scene,
The cheeps and peeps and chirrups silenc'd, calm.
E'en birds do rest their speeding hearts at times,
Their feathers fallow 'til another flight.
Within this nest, the hurlyburly's done,   5
For many battles have been lost and won,
And there shall be more with the rising sun.
Inside our Globe, there is not time enow
For these, our noble actors, to portray
The other acts, the settings and the plots,   10
The characters—their entrances and exits—
Of our dramatic, troubl'd history.
For now, then, be at peace with one another,
And if ye should have need of quick McTweet,
Remember, I am there to be your voice—   15
Your plumèd messenger shall gladly sing
Whate'er frustrations or complains you have
As you behold our governmental woes.
For now, let us return to greater things,
And fly once more on better angels' wings.   20

                               [Exit.

END.

AFTERWORD.

As with many collaborations, this one is made of several stories. Ian started his in 1977, and Giacomo Calabria (aka "Jacopo") followed suit seven years later. Ian grew up in the '80s, and Jacopo the '90s. Ian watched *G. I. Joe*, and Jacopo watched *X-Men*. Ian played Nintendo, and Jacopo played Sega. We both loved *The Simpsons* and *Star Wars* and can recite *The Princess Bride* from memory. And yes, we're both glad that being a nerd is cool these days.

Enter England's top nerd, William Shakespeare.

In July 2018, Ian read Jacopo's novel *License to Quill*, a James Bond/William Shakespeare mashup that was right up Ian's alley. When the story ended, Ian found Jacopo online and sent him a message of appreciation. Jacopo, who was an admirer of Ian's William Shakespeare's Star Wars series, wrote back a few hours later. Our correspondence quickly developed into a friendship because we respected each other as both readers and writers.

These conversations soon turned to collaboration. We'd both had ideas for a Shakespearean-style history play set in the modern era—specifically, during the presidential administration of Donald Trump. We developed a story that we called *MacTrump*, which was originally planned with two endings: one comic and one tragic. Given the ever-changing political climate, that story needed to be reworked regularly. Our manuscript became a living document. We even accidentally predicted the future a few times!

We pitched our story to Quirk Books, and here we are.

In many ways, this book is the natural combination of our separate lives and talents. Jacopo is a former staffer for the Barack Obama presidential campaign. Ian is the author of ten books written in Shakespeare's style. We both brought to this project a deep interest in Shakespeare, politics, history, literature, and popular culture. We also had a decent understanding of how Shakespeare wrote his plays—with and without Christopher Marlowe's help, it's now safe to say. We traded scenes to write, edited everything together, and ended up with what is ultimately a representative mix of our viewpoints and writing styles. It is our closest approximation to the musings of a nonthreatening ghost of Shakespeare.

We made many decisions along the way as we condensed so much history into a fictional five-act parody. You'll notice that, with the exception of a czar named Putain, our story focuses almost entirely on domestic affairs. Characters had to be cut—members of Congress suffered the most in this regard. Conversely, we added references to historical figures, symbols, and literary works from U.S. history that we think Shakespeare would have included.

In telling a modern story in a Shakespearean context, we had to decide how to handle anachronisms. We wanted to stay away from mentions of specific technology, but we did include objects, words, and expressions that didn't exist in Shakespeare's time. You won't find a cell phone or a computer in our story, but you will find references to things that happened long after Shakespeare lived. Of course, Shakespeare had no problem including clocks in *Julius Caesar* or writing about the paranormal. We faced a complicated and captivating dilemma that forced us to explore questions that are, frankly, fun to ask: Would Shakespeare have used Twitter? Would he have been a hipster? Where would he buy his coffee? Would he have been a Slytherin? Would the Bard of Avon have been a fan of *Game of Thrones*? If so, how would he have streamed it: on a magic mirror or a writing tablet? Most important, what would Shakespeare have thought of the contemporary United States?

Our hope is that this book allows you, the reader, to explore the first two years of the Trump presidency, so you can learn from it and laugh at it, no differently from the regulars in the Globe Theatre. We hope you remember the best and worst of those years, yes, but also reprocess them in a way that leaves you laughing—or at least thinking— instead of crying. Even Shakespeare's darkest acts had life to them, and their beating heart echoes across the world's stage every day.

Inevitably, by the time you read this, even more history will have been made. Be assured that, whatever happens next, we will be on hand to reenvision it, mock it, and turn it into high drama as only Shakespeare—or, in this case, two Shakespeare nerds—could do.

ACKNOWLEDGMENTS.

FROM ID:

Thank you to my Jennifer, spouse extraordinaire, and to my kids Liam and Graham—I hope your generation does better than mine. To my parents Bob and Beth Doescher, my brother Erik, his wife Em, and my nieces Aracelli and Addison. To Josh Hicks, Alexis Kaushansky, Tom George, Kristin Gordon George, Chloe Ackerman, Graham Steinke, Ethan Youngerman, Heidi Altman, Naomi Walcott, and Chris Martin. And to everyone else I name in every book—thank you all so, so much. And of course, to Giacomo, my coauthor extraordinaire, thank you for a whirlwind of collaboration that has been a true joy.

FROM JDQ:

My deepest thanks to Ian for surprising me with such kind words about *License to Quill* last year! I always admired you as a writer, but thank you for the added reasons to admire you as a friend, a writing partner, and a person. To my fiancée Taylor for her encouragement and musings, to my parents Joe and Anna, and all my family and friends. Special thanks to Ray Errol Fox, Jonathan Maberry, Dr. Rae Muhlstock and Dan, Geoffrey Sheehan, Edwin Thrower, the Frank J. Basloe Library, the Albany Public Library, everyone I worked with in 2008, and all my readers and followers.

FROM BOTH OF US:

To the team at Quirk Books, especially our editor Jhanteigh Kupihea, assistant editor Rebecca Gyllenhaal, publicity mavens Nicole De Jackmo and Ivy Weir, and copy phenom Jane Morley. To everyone who thinks we can, should, and must do better—let's come together in 2020.

SONNET 1202021

"The Internet Is Yuge"

My country, 'tis of thee this tale was writ,
And though the story pauseth, life goes on.
MacMueller did his narrative submit,
Which makes the family MacTrump withdrawn.
More of the story we'll not tell for now,
Until the history itself is made.
Yet if some further hijinks you'll allow,
There's more upon the internet display'd—
Unto **quirkbooks.com** hie ye with pride,
Where you may other interests pursue:
There ye shall find *MacTrump: The Readers Guide*,
And read an **interview** with authors two.
Whether you sit to left or right of th'aisle,
The Quirk Books website shall cause you to smile.

www.quirkbooks.com/mactrump